A MOST LIKELY TO NOVEL

CANDY SLOANE

This book is a work of fiction. Names, characters, places, and incidents are the product of the author's imagination or are used fictitiously. Any resemblance to actual events, locales, or persons, living or dead, is coincidental.

Copyright © 2016 by Candy Sloane. All rights reserved, including the right to reproduce, distribute, or transmit in any form or by any means. For information regarding subsidiary rights, please contact the Publisher.

Entangled Publishing, LLC
2614 South Timberline Road
Suite 109
Fort Collins, CO 80525
Visit our website at www.entangledpublishing.com.

Brazen is an imprint of Entangled Publishing, LLC. For more information on our titles, visit www.brazenbooks.com.

Edited by Stacy Abrams
Cover design by Heather Howland
Cover art from iStock

Manufactured in the United States of America

First Edition March 2016

Chapter One

Valerie had hit empty on her daily supply of exasperated groans. Over the past three hours, Alec's lateness had ratcheted up from charming to maddening to code-red-level dick. Hanging out in baggage claim with her elbow propped on her upended suitcase and her face in her hand wasn't how she'd planned on starting her high school reunion weekend.

Her chin was going numb and her neck ached. She shifted position and glanced down. While it alleviated her pain, the view rekindled it. Hours of waiting had wreaked wrinkled havoc on her tan linen skirt and fitted white button down.

She was going to kill him.

Her silent phone mocked her, though she was thankful for the excuse to have it glued to her hand. She'd been stalking her inbox all day for an email from the London Philharmonic.

She couldn't will an acceptance email for their year-long residency program into her inbox any more than she could check one of the arrival screens for an update on where the hell Alec was. He was traveling by private plane—a smirk tugged at her lips—just like anyone would to his ten-year high school reunion.

Alec had taken the time they spent hanging out in the Kenmore High School band room and become the lead singer and lead guitarist of the Grammy-winning rock band Chronic Disharmony. Valerie had taken it and become the second flute chair for the Philadelphia Philharmonic.

For now. She snuck another furtive glance at her inbox.

She and Alec had been so similar in high school—Val and Al—but they were polar opposites now, at least in the music world. *Well,* Valerie seethed as more minutes ticked by, *in etiquette, too.*

She noticed a lanky guy with brown hair in the distance and perked up—*finally*—but the relaxed smile she'd pasted on as camouflage before she ripped Alec a new one stiffened.

It wasn't him.

She crossed her arms and grumbled. Apparently he was going for induction into the *Penis's World Record Book.*

She had timed their expected arrivals to coincide with dinner. Walking in fashionably late would assure that the people she wanted to avoid would be occupied. But now, the Opening Night Dinner had long since ended. Her stomach clawed and whimpered. She riffled through her carry-on for the last of her plane peanuts.

She hadn't seen Alec in person since they'd graduated from Kenmore High, but lately his face had been everywhere: on TV, all over the internet, and on the cover of the magazine jutting out from her purse. She'd been browsing the airport newsstand in Philly before her flight when she saw him: Alec Rogers, her best friend, on the cover of *Rolling Stone.* They'd poured him into leather pants and nothing else. The museum of tattoos on his chest and shoulders was framed by taut arms. Two ladder rungs of ab muscles laced up his stomach, a concave at his belly button the perfect size for some lucky lady's lips.

She shook her head, a stress headache nipping at her temples. *Why am I thinking about that?*

Maybe because she'd bought the copy of *Rolling Stone* to give Alec crap about being such a rock star pretty boy, but instead she'd stared at it, at *him*, from the time she boarded the plane until she had reached cruising altitude. It might have ended up with a ring of drool around that belly button had the flight attendant not interrupted to see if she wanted a drink.

She had. Vodka straight.

Her phone finally dinged with a text from Alec.

You busy?

It was the same message he sent her daily, usually after midnight. She had thousands just like it and thousands of other texts from him filling her phone like confetti.

No, she typed, her fingers taut with annoyance, *just waiting at the airport for some dick who's more than three hours late.*

"Want me to kick his ass?"

She knew that rough song-worn voice, knew the composed breath that waited for her response. Alec stood above her. As she took him in, her stomach seemed to float up like a balloon she'd just let go of—a cocktail of excitement and nervousness buzzing and zinging as it launched into her throat.

His signature dark brown fauxhawk was hidden under a baseball cap, his torso and arm tattoos shielded by a leather jacket. But it was *him*, her Al, and at the same time it wasn't. His combat boots made him appear taller than she remembered, and his shoulders seemed broader, even more so than when she'd seen them bare on the cover of *Rolling Stone*.

She finally remembered to smile, to do something other than stare.

His kind brown eyes lit up. "Val." He set down his guitar case and pulled her into an embrace so forceful she almost lost one of her pumps.

He smelled of leather and alcohol, of a rock star.

"Al," she replied, hugging him back. Forgetting her annoyance for the moment and remembering how they did this—said each other's names with different inflection dependent on their mood.

She snuggled into him. The slight frame he'd had in high school was as well-built as it looked. Her abdomen stiffened against the muscles of his own. The stubble on his chin bristled at her cheek.

"I'll do it," he said. "I'm just trying to figure out how you kick a dick's ass. Does it even have one?"

"I don't know. Maybe we should ask the dick."

He let out a dry laugh. "I'm sorry I'm late." He squeezed her again. "If Dante were still with us, he would agree that L.A. traffic should be the tenth circle of hell."

"I'd nominate high school reunions for that illustrious spot." Her stomach pitched. She'd hated having to wait all those hours for Alec, but now that he was here, they would have to go to the reunion. See all those people from high school. Worse, they would see her. "I can't believe you convinced me to come to this thing," she continued. She parsed out her anxiety from the dizziness of talking to Alec in person, being in his arms. Her heart panted like a dog begging for a treat. She forced herself to let go of him.

"Val, we've made good. We deserve to be here."

He certainly had. She wasn't so sure about herself. She used to be a girl who played flute, and now she was a woman who did. While Alec's star had risen, hers had barely even begun to gather up the dust to be born.

He inclined his head at her purse. "I see you got my *Rolling Stone* debut. Isn't it awesome?"

"Ten more minutes of waiting and I was going to draw donkey ears and domino-sized teeth on it."

Alec's mouth curved into a knowing smile. "Like we used to do to yearbook photos of people we didn't like. I know I was late, but you still like me, don't you?" His voice was thick, pointed.

He had the same gentle face she knew, the same wide jaw and honest chin, but there was a hint of something mischievous behind his eyes. Alec had always had that to some degree, but now he had the swagger and sex appeal to match. The way his brown eyes sampled hers, the way his body shielded her view from everything in the world but him—it was unsettling and not at all the way she expected to feel around him. The discrepancy almost made her stumble.

"You're not remembering right. It was people we thought were asses," she corrected, "and three hours late, that makes you officially an ass." One of the pictures from his magazine spread flashed into her mind—Alec, his strong back to the camera, a guitar sandwiched between his legs and his plump figure-eight ass in those leather pants. It was enough to give any woman daydreams for days, fantasies forever. But not her—she was not supposed to be thinking about that. She blinked, bringing herself back to the real thing standing right in front of her.

"I know it might seem dumb to someone waiting to hear about a chair in the London Philharmonic, but I'm proud of making the cover." He pointed at the magazine again.

"It doesn't seem dumb," she admitted.

Their gaze held. She considered telling him she was proud of him, too, but he knew. He knew every little thing her mind ever thought. She winced, hoping he'd missed the whole figure-eight ass in leather pants segment.

"Let's get the car before someone recognizes you," he finally said, leading her out of the airport.

A black Maserati convertible as dark as the night sky above sat out front waiting for them.

"They shipped it up for me special," Alec said as he opened Valerie's door. The inside reminded her of her flute case, black and soft. Valerie had known the minute she'd seen him, but sitting in this two-hundred-thousand-dollar car, there was no doubt Alec was a rock star. Successful beyond even the dreams he'd shared with her while they lay on the carpet of her high school bedroom staring up at the glow-in-the-dark stars on her ceiling.

"It's amazing, but a bit much for Kenmore, don't you think?" she said as he started the engine.

Alec had removed his hat and leather jacket. A white T-shirt played tug of war with his pectoral muscles and was losing. The tattoos she'd studied on the cover of *Rolling Stone* were like pieces of artwork in person—a wing emerging from his left elbow, black feathers exploding up and down his arm. A black vine of thorns wrapping up his right, binding against his taut, solid…

"Wait until you see the suite I got us. Three bedrooms, two bathrooms." He beamed, waking her from her trance, the dimple that fans fainted over peeking through.

She'd agreed without question when Alec suggested they room together for the reunion. But how could she have anticipated being near him would make her feel this way? Tongue-tied, nervous, confused as hell…and a little turned on. In high school, they would lie next to each other on her bed for hours talking, the thought of touching him never crossing her mind—but now that thought needed an army of crossing guards.

"Things must have changed a lot since high school. I can't believe hotels in Kenmore have suites now."

"The Sheraton is the poshest hotel in Kenmore."

"Now that's an oxymoron."

His eyes scraped boldly over her. "Doesn't mean I can't throw a little money around for you, does it, Val?"

She shifted in her seat, hoping the thrum she sensed between her legs was just the roar of the engine.

"I'm surprised you didn't bring a date." She'd not only seen Alec all over the media alone, but with women, lots of them, each one as much like artwork as his tattoos.

Valerie, on the other hand, had dated exactly three guys since high school: one throughout college, one six months after she graduated, and the last, Charles, she'd broken up with because he couldn't commit to marrying her. He used to say: "The word commit makes me think of an insane asylum."

Valerie understood. Trying to get Charles to comply had made her feel like she was locked up and straight-jacketed in one, but she had learned her lesson. Keeping an unwilling man was like keeping a bird. You just ended up with an empty cage and a bunch of crap you had to clean up.

No more. Hopefully she would move to London and never look back. Still, she couldn't help staring at her naked finger. A ring was supposed to be the frosting on the cake of the woman she was now. Without it, she had no physical proof that men actually found her attractive. That she wasn't the same girl she used to be in high school.

"I'm surprised you didn't bring your flute," Alec finally replied as they pulled onto the Thruway.

Her cheeks bloomed despite the evening wind. "Hilarious." Valerie's teeth felt too big for her mouth, even though this was where their conversations went eventually—slid into jokes about their sex lives. Val's "boring" one and Alec's "excessively hot" one. "The next time you masturbate with your guitar, call me," she continued, trying to keep up.

Alec opened his mouth to speak and then closed it.

"You like to keep that stuff private?" she pressed, pleased she was winning this round.

He glanced at her, his eyes sharp. "Watching is optional, but once you do, participation is mandatory."

Her heart seemed to stammer, her lungs suddenly an inferno. Wow, she was not even close to winning. Lava spread up her belly, wound around her neck. She searched her mind for a response.

"Besides, I probably won't need my guitar for that this weekend," he said. "I'm thinking I'll find someone at the reunion."

She sensed a lump in her throat, but there was relief, too. He might look different, her body might be reacting differently, but he was Alec and she was Valerie. They were being Al and Val. She just wasn't used to jousting with him when he was so close. All their conversations since high school had been virtual; they'd just have to learn how to be physical again.

Physical?

She fought wooziness at her slip. Not that kind of physical. There was no doubt being inches from a man who millions of women wanted was making her delirious. Or maybe it wasn't Alec at all. She hadn't touched anyone but herself since she and Charles broke up three months ago. She was bound to have booty on the brain.

"Well, if you bring someone back to the room," she finally replied, lifting the hair off her neck, needing the tickle of cool air, "put a necktie on the door or something to warn me."

"Maybe that's what they use in the Symphony; rock stars go with a bra."

"Classy."

"Why change what works?"

Valerie couldn't deny, even though it was baffling the hell out of her, that this new Alec worked.

He took his hand off the wheel and lowered it, his fingers hovering inches from her bare knee. Her skin prickled, goose bumps screaming to life. He changed gears and gripped the wheel again. The breath she hadn't realized she'd been holding burst out. Wow, this was going to be one long weekend.

They entered the yawning mouth of suburban Kenmore, NY. Strip malls and Starbucks reigned with farms and the start of New England woods sprinkled around for greenery. Valerie hadn't been back in five years, since her parents followed the migration of most of the older set from their temple and moved to Florida. Even in the dark, the suburban status quo had changed very little.

Alec parked at the hotel and began to exit the car, but Valerie paused. He would get a king's welcome, but she would still be the same band-geek Valerie she was ten years ago.

"You're not seriously nervous, are you?" Alec grabbed her upper arm, his rings pressing through the fabric of her shirt and into her skin.

"No." Valerie sighed. But she was. All her old insecurities came flooding back—dorky, knock-kneed, stringy-haired Valerie, the kind of girl who could only get lucky with her flute.

His chestnut eyes held her gaze. "Just follow my lead."

"You mean until you find the person wearing the bra you're going to hang on our door knob." Her lower lip quivered slightly.

He squared his hand tight on her shoulder, his eyes deepening. "There's no Al without Val."

It was what people used to say about them back in high school. They were inseparable besties. One was never without the other. Well, at least they had been until the day after graduation—the day it took Alec years to forgive her for.

Who would have known that ten years later she would be struggling to stop picturing him with his shirt off? Maybe it was good that once they were finally talking and texting again, life got in the way of them visiting each other.

She blew her bangs up. *One issue at a time*.

"If you hate it, we can go to the room and watch movies like we used to in high school."

"It'll be fine." Nothing was like it used to be in high school. If she had trouble being in the car with Alec, being alone in a room with him "watching movies" was out of the question.

"I can make it fin*er*," Alec said, digging into the center console and unearthing a metal flask. He swayed it in front of her, hypnotist style. "It's vodka, your favorite."

She shook her head. She'd had a drink on the plane, but they were here now. She was with him now. She'd need her wits about her, that was for sure.

He unscrewed the top, brought it to his lips, and took a long gulp. He grimaced slightly but didn't cough. "You want to go into your high school reunion sober, that's your choice." His voice was syrupy from the liquor. "But there is no way in hell I'm facing those jackals unarmed."

He had a point.

...

Alec watched Val take a long, determined sip. Her lips teased the mouth of the flask, her throat opened and closed for a good five seconds. She must have learned to handle her liquor since high school. He remembered a similar scene starring a bottle of pilfered gin in her backyard gazebo sophomore year. The night had ended with them hosing out the gazebo, hosing off each other, and finally running around the yard in the summer dark having a water fight.

If he'd been trading gin shots with one of the women he spent time with now, that scene would have ended with them wet and naked and fucking. But he had been a different boy then—shy, quiet, insecure—and Valerie one of his only friends.

He and Valerie *only* friends.

He hadn't thought about that night in years, and he definitely hadn't replayed it with a XXX filter, ever. He wondered if it was because of how much he'd changed, or because when he saw Valerie waiting in baggage claim, instead of running to greet her, he found himself pausing and staring—amazed and speechless that the girl who had never even seemed like a girl to him was such a woman now.

She'd had one heel off, her chocolate brown bangs in her eyes, a pale pink bra peeping out from her button down when the light hit it just right. She was his Val, but she was also her own woman. A woman if he'd met in a bar now, he would have made sure they ended the night wet and naked and fucking.

She lowered the flask, her eyes watering and her neck tight. She wanted to cough but was holding it in. He laughed. Not at her, but because he missed this—the two of them just being the two of them. "You don't have to prove anything to me, remember?"

"Thank," she croaked, a string of coughs exploding from her like the *rat-tat-tat* of a machine gun, "God."

He snuck a glance at the way her tits pitched and fought against her white shirt as she caught her breath. Almost choking to death wasn't sexy, and Val definitely was not supposed to be, but there was something about the way she kept herself so buttoned up that intrigued him.

The women he partied with since Chronic Disharmony became a household name did not wear button-down shirts, and if they did, they were his. Usually the morning after, open and framing their curves while they beckoned him for round two, or three, or four.

He lifted the flask to his mouth and took a burning swig. While he saw that in his mind, it wasn't a specific memory. All those women were running together now, all those nights, all those drinks.

The single anchor was Valerie. The only person in the world he could count on—his one constant. Even back in high school when things with his dad got to be too much, he had

Valerie. He had her room where he slept on her floor until his father calmed down, if he ever calmed down.

She'd always been there for him. He shouldn't have been staring at her tits. Staring would inevitably lead to wanting. He couldn't go down that road with her. She deserved better than a meaningless fuck with a rock star.

He focused back on the flask. "More?"

"Maybe in a minute," she replied. "I can't believe I took four days out of my life for this."

He put the cap back on and set it down. "I'm counting and I'm only up to three."

Though even three days was a long time to be back in his hometown. Of course, he wasn't just here for this, or for her. He planned to check on the house he'd purchased for his mother on Niagara Road that he still couldn't convince her to move into. He'd been trying for a year with no luck. She'd agreed to come back to Kenmore, but not without the man who'd made his life hell for eighteen years.

"Not everyone can call their private jet to come and pick them up the minute they're done Sunday night."

"They can't?" He shoved the flask at her. "You need to drink more. We both do."

"I'm not about to say yes to everything you ask, Alec."

He already knew that. It was one of the reasons they were still best friends. She was always truthful, real. He wondered if some of their closeness came from the fact they were both only children—she because her parents wanted one perfect child and he because he suspected his father hadn't wanted him at all. His head pounded, the phantom pain of his father's blows pelting down like it did from time to time when he thought about him.

It was why he avoided thinking about him. Why he avoided everything. Why he had the flask that Valerie was still squinting at.

He set it down. Her friendship was a salve, too, and he hoped being near her would keep the barrage of memories at bay. He reached for his phone. There was a text from his manager about a contract negotiation and an email from his publicist stating the paparazzi didn't know he was at the reunion as of yet but who knew how long that would last.

Nothing that couldn't wait, so he put it away. He realized Val hadn't checked her phone since he arrived, which seemed odd to him. There were people in her world besides him, most recently her boyfriend Charles, a vice president at a shipping and packaging company.

"What's Mr. Peanut doing this weekend? Aren't you guys engaged by now?"

She sighed and rolled her eyes.

He loved how the name he'd chosen for Charles based on the Styrofoam peanuts his company used by the truckload made her bristle. He'd also chosen it for what he hoped was the size of his dick.

"Where are the other guys in the band this weekend? Aren't you married by now?"

She was deflecting, but fine, he'd play along. "Since we're not starting our new album until fall and our next tour isn't until after the holidays, we're on hiatus. I think Jessie is in Ibiza, Ryan is at his lake house in Tahoe, and Scott is working his way through the single Kardashian sisters. Do you need me to continue, or are you going to stop avoiding my question?"

She took an immersive breath, like she needed fuel to keep talking. "I broke up with him."

They sat in silence for a moment, until Alec realized she wasn't going to keep going without a push. "Is that the whole story?"

She forced her eyes into her lap. "He didn't want to marry me"—she paused—"now or ever. That's the whole story." She managed to look up at him with a scowl. "I know you think marriage is a joke."

Valerie knew better than anyone that the M word made him laugh and laugh. Considering the family he came from, it was either laugh and laugh or cry and cry, and he'd chosen not to dwell but to dodge. Valerie, however, had bought the fairy tale; she believed in forever.

"It's not a joke to you," he said quietly.

"That doesn't sound like a compliment."

At this point he wasn't sure what it was. When he'd attempted to offer her forever the day after graduation, she'd rejected him. But he hadn't asked her to get married. He'd asked her to move to New York City. It had been impulsive and stupid and made him even less of a fan of the word "forever" now than he was then.

It took almost two years for him to be able to take her calls after that, but in the end he was glad she'd been smart enough to see what he'd blinded himself to. He hadn't been asking her to come with him because he couldn't live without her. He had been asking because he was afraid to be alone.

"It's not like I'm about to buy a mail-order groom or anything. I just want to finally find a man who is willing to make sacrifices for me."

"Easier said than done, huh?"

She sighed. "Maybe I would do better with a mail-order groom."

"I'm sorry," he said, though he was and he wasn't. He'd never met Mr. Peanut, but he was clearly a total douche. Anyone who didn't want to marry Val would have to be. *Just look at her.* And in that moment he realized he was. The dark sky seemed an extension of her long, dark-umber hair, the skin of her heart-shaped face rivaled the moonlight, and her caramel-colored eyes pulsated with the heat of stars.

Fuck, he needed to stop.

She was telling him she broke up with a guy who couldn't

commit, and he was gawking at her like she was one of his groupies. He put a pause on his thoughts before he compared her tits to distant planets or something.

"So, are you okay?" he asked.

"Yeah." She looked away. "It was three months ago."

Three months ago? A vise went to work in his chest. They had spoken, texted, or FaceTimed almost every day. Why hadn't she said something? Was she embarrassed?

She finally turned back. "I know, I know," she said, holding up a hand, "I should have told you. He didn't even have the balls to do it in person."

His body tensed. "Forget about the dick who kept you waiting at the airport. Now, I want to kick *his* ass."

"He's not worth it," she said, her eyes downturned. "You don't have to make a big show."

"It's because I care, Val." He pictured stuffing Mr. Peanut's mouth full of that Styrofoam shit until he choked on it.

"I know." She leaned back in the seat.

The buttons at the top of her shirt stretched open. The view of curved, soft skin combined with vodka was making him lightheaded.

"Seems like you're the only one who does sometimes," she added.

It was how he felt, too, and was all the more reason he needed to stop staring at her tits. Needed to remember that the kind of man who should be staring at them was someone who could give her what she wanted—a ring, a house, a life.

"At least now you can get some while you're here," he said, desperate to bring back the balance of them—Al and Val, joking, playing, giving each other shit. It was what he would have said to one of the guys in the band after a breakup. It was what he should say to his best friend regardless of how great her tits were.

She crossed her legs, her skirt applying a dangerous line

on her thighs. "With who? The only guy I talked to in all of high school was you."

The back of his neck burned. Did he want her to be with anyone else when he was in ass-kicking distance? Hell no. But he couldn't say that. He wouldn't say that, so instead he said, "We're different people now."

"You are. You'll have every woman in our class lining up. Knowing Reece, she has a sign-up sheet going already for her pretty friends."

He laughed. Reece Freedland, valedictorian, planner extraordinaire, and one of the most popular girls in school. He thought of the itinerary she'd sent via snail mail. Everything had been scheduled for the weekend down to the millisecond. Hell, she probably did have a sign-up sheet.

"I can teach you my ways." He lifted his brows up and down comically. "The best way to get over a breakup is to fuck someone new."

"Thanks, Confucius."

"That's Cock-fucius," he tossed back with a wicked grin.

She shook her head. "I can only imagine what your fortune cookies might say."

He opened his mouth to reply, and she pressed a hand over it.

"If you say *it's fortune nookie* you get a punch to your namesake."

He swallowed a laugh. She knew him too well.

"Besides," she said, removing her hand, "I'm over it. Like I said, it's been three months."

She was lying. She might have been over Mr. Peanut, but she was not over wanting what she must have thought he could promise her.

"I'm done with men," she announced, as if sensing his train of thought.

One side of his mouth perked up. "See, you *have* changed

since high school."

"That's not what I meant!" She slapped his knee. It was innocent, but her touch felt anything but, considering what they were talking about.

"Just because you're done with men doesn't mean you're done with sex, right?"

"I'm dejected, not dead." She threw her head back, exposing the soft skin of her neck.

His mouth watered. He forced himself to take a swig from the flask, trying to dull his taste buds. "You need to find someone to fuck Mr. Peanut out of you."

He thought she'd say *forget it*, and he wanted her to. *What the hell am I doing?* He was going to find someone to fuck her? This had gone sideways fast. But what else could he do, fuck her himself?

He couldn't. He shouldn't. No matter how goddamn hot she was now, he wouldn't. She was not just some woman he could fuck and leave. She was the one person who'd made his life livable in high school—the one person who knew all his secrets and didn't judge him now.

He couldn't fuck that up with sex.

And who said she was interested anyway? He might be able to get any woman he wanted, but that didn't mean he could get Valerie. She hadn't taken him seriously in high school and there was no way she would now. She was out of his league—beautiful, successful, driven, and, most importantly, his best friend.

She seemed to ponder his suggestion. "Who?"

Fuck my stupid man-advice. Now we're doing this.

"It doesn't matter, really." He took another swig from the flask in the hopes it might make his words appear genuine. "But since I'm here, I'll help you pick him out."

"Won't you be too busy finding someone for yourself?"

"I'm not here for them, Val. I'm here for you." The way

her eyes dampened let him know he needed to keep talking. "It'll be fun." If she wanted his help, he would give it to her. Get her a guy to make that faraway look disappear, if only for the night.

"Finding me someone to *fuck* the Mr. Peanut out of me will be fun?" She smirked.

He knew she was only repeating what he'd said, but hearing her voice around that word was something he felt in every cell in his body, every beat of his suddenly off-the-charts pounding heart. "Do you want to get him out of your system or not?" he asked, trying to shake the hum in his veins.

She reached for the flask and took a long swig. "Looks like I'm going to need a necktie for our doorknob."

Chapter Two

Val was wobbly as they headed inside the hotel. She should never have told Alec about Charles. It was embarrassing—a man who she'd given years to running away rather than granting her forever. There must have been something seriously wrong with her.

Considering Alec thought she needed help getting laid, was there any doubt?

But fine, she'd accept his assistance. Maybe it was the vodka talking, but she could definitely handle some casual sex. Especially since it was one of the only things on her mind since Alec arrived—since she saw that *Rolling Stone* cover.

Better it be with someone who she never had to talk to again after this weekend.

They found the ballroom where the Opening Night Dinner was being held. Out front a table was littered with the remnants of name tags. Valerie spied hers and was thankful it was spelled correctly: *Valerie Barkin*.

Some of the popular kids had started calling her *Barking* freshman year, as in *woof woof*, as in dog, as in ugly. The addition of just that one letter had turned her into an easy target.

Nice flute solo, Barking; your turn at the board, Barking; you dropped your pen, Barking. She shuddered. She was usually able to push the memories out of her mind, but not when she was about to face some of those people again.

She ran a hand through her hair, popped a mint in her mouth, and said a little prayer as they walked into the ballroom.

The dinner had pretty much dissipated. The tables were cleared, and the bar was empty. Only a small group of their ex-classmates sat in a circle toward the front of the room. Valerie was surprised to see people from every clique gathered, including her good friend Cynthia from band, who had also played flute.

She and Cynthia caught up while everyone fawned over Alec. Cynthia was a music teacher now—divorced, but happily. The blond hair she wore like Rapunzel in high school was in an asymmetrical bob, and her navy blue eyes were blurry with drunkenness.

Turned out everyone was drunk, and after a few sloppy hugs and squeals, the attention was off of Alec and back on the game they had interrupted: Seven Minutes in Heaven.

She waved to Cynthia. "I'll see you at breakfast tomorrow."

Alec grabbed her arm, whispered, "This is your chance."

"Now?" Sure, she'd accepted his offer to help, but they'd been here ten minutes. "I'm tired," she added when he still hadn't released her arm.

"Cock-fucius say, *fuck first, sleep later.*"

She glanced around the circle, reading the name tags of the men who used to be boys. None of them had been more to her than a body in the hallway during high school. She supposed any one of them could just as easily be a body in the dark.

She shrugged. Might as well get it over with. She grabbed a chair and pulled it into the circle. She'd take Alec's suggestion, but she was not sitting on the floor in a tan skirt.

"Alec," Randy Tines slurred, indicating the bottle in the center of the circle, "you take a spin. I'm sure all these ladies want a piece of the famous rock star in the dark." Randy had been the high school yearbook photographer, and he took his skills to manage a bank.

"With a lady in the dark is my favorite place to be."

Valerie wanted to scoff, but she couldn't. The way his voice deepened around those words made her shiver, her abdomen contract.

"But I think Val should go first," he suggested. Alec stared at her, his eyes impatient. He was taking this Cockfucius thing way too seriously.

"She can just go after you, Alec," Jenny Gordon pressed. She was an ex–volleyball star, current gym teacher, who looked like she'd had two fully inflated Spaldings implanted in her chest since graduation. She hadn't even known Alec's name in high school.

"Whatever, someone go." Randy Tines spun a finger in the air.

Alec smirked at Valerie, his damn dimple coming out. She felt like she might melt, a puddle on the chair in just her button down and knee-length skirt.

"Fine," Valerie proclaimed. She took a deep breath and spun. Watched the bottle go from Randy to Kenneth to Jacob to Alec to Paul back to Randy and on and on in a kinky kaleidoscope she had no control over.

When it finally landed, she almost fell out of her chair. It pointed right in the middle of the crossed legs of Alec's distressed jeans. Her cheeks lit up, and her heart knocked against her rib cage as if it were asking if anyone was still alive in there.

Jenny looked like one of her implants had exploded. Even though Valerie was dealing with her own inner meltdown, she said a silent *woo-hoo*.

Cynthia covered her mouth, but it was clear she was smiling.

"Let's go, you two," Randy pushed.

Valerie waited for something, for anything. Sure, she'd been thinking about touching Alec, about Alec touching her, but this was real. This was happening.

"Maybe I should spin again," she suggested, her heartbeat drowning out the sound of her own voice.

"The bottle chooses," Jacob Riedel, ex high school soccer star, current sports equipment store owner, said, shaking his head. "We don't choose."

Clearly this decree had been tossed to a couple already who had been unhappy with their result, but no one sitting around this circle had as much to lose by going into that closet together as Valerie and Alec did.

"Rules are rules," Alec said with a shrug.

Even *he* wasn't going to help her.

The room whirled at the speed of that damn bottle, but when Alec finally stood and held out his hand, to Valerie's surprise, she took it.

• • •

"What the hell was that?" Val's eyes were shiny in the half light of the janitor's closet. "You should have let me spin again."

Alec leaned against the closed door. "Those guys were assholes. None of them deserves to breathe on you, let alone fuck you." He smelled peppermint and sensed the heat of Val's body. It was an unsettling combination—alluringly unsettling—ice hot.

They'd always talked to each other about everything. She could give him shit like no one else, but there was something bubbling below their usual ribbing, their usual heart to heart— want, need, *this*.

"You're the one who said I should play, Cock-fucius," she spit.

The friend in him had suggested it, but when the bottle spun and one of the guys in that circle got that much closer to Valerie, the man in him won out.

"What are we supposed to do now?" she asked.

It was the question in his head, too, and he forced himself to keep asking it, because the only answer that kept lighting up, *give in to the whole heaven part of this game*, could not happen. So why was he tempting himself?

"We don't have to do anything." Though with nothing between them but anticipation and air, he wasn't sure how long that might last.

"I probably couldn't have gone through with it anyway." She chuckled with relief. Her throaty laugh was dizzying, beckoning.

"With anyone?" He edged closer. His heart thumped, roared like a lion with each increasing inch. *What the hell am I doing?*

Having her in the dark, alone, was like giving him permission. The fact that she stood her ground as he stepped closer was giving him a purpose.

He shouldn't want this. She was his best friend. But he couldn't stop.

Even in the dark, he could sense her curves. Ample breasts just begging for a skimpy tank top, her ass plump in that tight little skirt and insistent for a strong squeeze, or a smack if she was being naughty.

The way her gaze locked and her breath met the speed of his own as he erased the last bit of space between them, he was sure she was naughty. Very naughty. That she would welcome the palm of his hand.

And just like that, his best friend had made him hard.

"I don't hear anything in there," Randy Tines yelled from outside the door.

"I think we're supposed to be kissing," Alec said, his cock so rigid he thought she could feel it through his pants.

"You mean each other?"

"We could just make kissing noises," he suggested, thinking of his lips teasing along the inside of her collar, biting off button after button of her shirt and spitting them out like watermelon seeds.

Hell yeah, he wanted to kiss her, her lips and her neck and the little spot behind her knee that she had been kneading as they drove here. He knew it was crazy, he knew it was wrong, but he wanted to be the guy to fuck Mr. Peanut out of her.

"Like this?" She pressed her hand to her lips and pretended to make out with it, her eyes on him as her tongue slicked over her skin.

His stomach rumbled in pure sexual hunger. One thing was for sure—all that flute practice had been good for a lot more than music.

"That sounds completely fake," he scoffed. Though considering the way his cock fought against the fabric of his pants, that was not entirely true.

Her bottom lip lay open against the inside of her palm. "You think you could do better?"

He yanked her hand to his lips before she could protest, before he could consider. He kissed it lightly at first, soft and drugging, slid the tip of his tongue up to her wrist, until he hit the buttoned cuff. "Maybe it should be me." The words spilled out against the soft-as-sin fabric.

"What?"

"Maybe I should be the one to fuck you like you deserve."

Val didn't reply, just breathed out more peppermint, hot peppermint against the skin of his face. Her eyes smoldered with want. It was clear she felt it, too, the heat between them, the confusing, beautiful, delicious heat.

He grabbed her forearm and drew her closer, slanting in to her chest. The shock of their bodies against each other caused them both to freeze. Not even a breath passed between them, but he knew exactly what he needed to do. He clenched the back of her head, and his lips dipped to her neck, dripping down her skin like melting ice. Fuck, he had to taste her. He opened his mouth, and his tongue lapped at her tender skin.

"Alec," she breathed.

"Follow my lead." He couldn't stop, though she certainly didn't seem like she was asking him to.

If anything, she was yielding to him. He trailed a finger down the center of her neck, playing with the top button of her shirt, pausing so he could think. Ten years. He could have gone to see her so many times. He hadn't at first because of how they'd left things after graduation, and then because their careers got in the way and they had both gotten into the routine of being like pen pals, but maybe he had really been avoiding their attraction.

There was no avoiding it now. There was no thinking. She needed this, and he was going to give it to her.

His hands rushed to her chest, undoing one button then another until her shirt was open and her pale pink bra was visible—her tits pumping up and down with deep, unsteady breaths.

Her fingers played with the bottom of his shirt.

"Take it off," he directed.

She heaved it over his head and ran her nails down the curves of his chest, her scratch creating an insatiable itch.

He slid his tongue against her clavicle, the hardness of it mirroring his own. The skin tasted like she smelled, like flowers in a vase, petals floating on water. He cupped his hand around her breast, and she yelped.

"Did I scare you?"

"Yes." She slipped her tongue into his ear. "Scare me again."

He teased at both her breasts, the delicate lace fabric in delicious opposition to her hard nipples. He circled his fingers around them slowly at first, then faster to meet her increasing gasps. She let out a slight moan like a whisper, like she was saying please.

Please.

She was so polite, even in her need.

He kissed the vertical line of her neck and continued to travel up. He still hadn't savored her lips.

The word "friend" should have stopped him, but they were in too deep now, and the word on his mind hadn't been friend—it had been fuck.

Fucking her—now.

"Two minutes," Randy yelled from outside the door.

A growl raged deep within. If he only had two more minutes, he was going to make the most of it. He clutched her ass with one hand and forced her skirt up with the other. The whine in her breath made his already hard cock throb.

Less than two minutes. Not enough time to fuck her properly, or even kiss her properly, but he couldn't stop.

And she couldn't, either. She thrust herself against his hand. Her movements were all instinct, all want. Just like his.

He trailed his fingers along her drenched lace panties. Holy fuck was she wet. He longed to slip them to the side and slide his cock deep. Take her slow, so slow they both wouldn't be able to stand it, before he slammed against her so relentlessly her breath broke. The whine at the back of her throat spiraling into a beg, a shriek, his name.

But this was Val, and they had a suite to share and a whole

weekend together. Did he really want to fuck her in a broom closet?

Hell yeah, he did, but she was his best friend.

But she was also a woman soaking through her panties for him, and he was a man holding what felt like the whole of the Capitol Records Building in his pants for her.

But she was also his best friend.

"We can do this, Val. But I need to hear the words. Do you want me to fuck you?" he rasped, pressing two fingers against the fabric over her clit.

Her breath vibrated on his lips, and she forced her hips closer so his fingers grazed her again.

"I can already feel how badly you want it. How wet and ready you are for me—"

"Alec," she interrupted, her voice begging.

With anyone else it would have been enough, but with her he had to hear it.

"Say it. Say you want me to fuck you," he insisted, wrapping his arms around her waist and pressing his cock against her thigh so viciously he could barely see.

Her mouth opened. She licked her lips, an eagerness in her eyes that made him want to enter her before she even had a chance to speak.

There was a knock at the door.

Val jumped away from him like a street cat that had been spooked.

"Time's up," Randy Tines yelled.

There was only their breath, so loud it drowned out everything. Her perfume was still on his lips, his cock strained against his pants. He waited for her to look at him, but she started to button up, avoiding his gaze.

"We should get dressed before someone comes in here," she finally said.

Alec adjusted himself as best he could and slipped his

shirt back on. His chest ached. His cock ached.

Maybe she hadn't wanted this? No, his fingers were still wet from her. Her body hadn't been the issue. Her mind must have woken up when she heard Randy's knock.

She bit her lip. "You ready?"

Her skittishness now, not the distance between them for the past ten years, was why they had never done this. Sex ruined friendships, especially when one of the friends knew he could never give more than friendship.

He nodded and she opened the door, light streaming in.

But she hadn't been asking for more. She'd been asking, begging, dripping for his cock. Fuck. He didn't want this to end because a stupid game said so, because Randy Tines said so.

He grabbed her wrist before she could exit, skated his lips against her ear. "You still need to answer my question."

Chapter Three

Valerie stood behind Alec at the sleek steel check-in desk dazed, drunk, and bursting with desire.

His question pulsed in her head. In every sensitive, swollen part of her, their contact had ignited. She would never have considered it a day ago. There wasn't a sinner's chance in heaven before the *Rolling Stone* cover, before that closet. Sure, she'd seen him when they FaceTimed and, of course, he'd been insanely hot for years, but not for her—never to her. He was Alec, her best friend, her buddy, and a man who fucked women like it was his job.

Alec. She'd turned his name into an entreaty for his touch. Warmth inundated the nape of her neck and dripped down. The way he'd looked at her, caressed her, taken charge of her, had changed the idea from *hell no* to a lot more than maybe.

Should he be the one? She let that thought swirl, but not before she amended it to: *for sex, anyway*.

But sex ruined friendships. It was a ubiquitous fact. She was surprised it wasn't one of the Ten Commandments. Somehow they worked past it in movies, but in real life it left friends enemies. In real life, people didn't declare their undying love to each other in a very public way with music, or flash mobs, or grand speeches.

Sure, she loved Alec and he loved her, but not like that. *Never* like that.

"Val."

She jumped, startled. Alec was snapping his fingers. How long had she been standing there?

"Is a room with a king bed okay?" He leaned against the check-in desk, but he was still tall enough to shield everything but him from her view.

"I thought you said we had a suite," she blurted. She'd been soothed knowing no matter what had happened in that closet, they had separate beds to sleep in, and doors they could close on each other.

"We did," he admitted, his brown eyes tense, "but they gave it away because we got in so late."

Valerie's heart spun. Usually a king bed would have been fine, but nothing was usual anymore.

"They don't have any double queen rooms left, either," Alec explained, scratching the back of his neck.

She'd touched him there and knew his hair was stiff with gel, stiff like... She shook her head. She hated that the number of beds was even an issue. There was a reason people always said sex ruined friendships. It had to be true, if almost-sex made things this awkward.

"Would you guys like a cot?" the lobby attendant asked.

"It's up to him," Valerie finally said. If he could control himself so could she, but if he couldn't...she was a goner.

"No, it's up to her," Alec retorted, not looking at her. He stood up straighter, faced the desk.

The lobby attendant swiveled his head from one of them to the other. "They're free if that's the issue."

Neither of them responded. Her throat burned. Her legs

tingled, but there was nowhere to run. This was crazy. Though she knew it wasn't all the almost-sex, it was just them being them. They made decisions together. Unlike some friendships she had with women who could be bossy or one-sided, she and Alec were equals.

Now they couldn't even make a simple choice about a crappy cot. They needed that cot, if for no other reason than to avoid similar standoffs.

Is this how our weekend will be now?

The lobby attendant typed on his keyboard. He went into the drawer at his desk and produced two key cards. He held one up in each hand. "Be sure to call down to the desk when you make up your minds," he added with a huge fake smile.

Smart-ass.

They each reached for a key and headed toward the elevator. Alec paused at the newsstand; the gate was down but the light inside was still on.

"Look." He pointed at the magazines. His *Rolling Stone* cover was stacked five across on the rack.

Even though staring at that cover had started this whole thing, she was thankful for the distraction now. "You didn't tell them to stock extra for this weekend, did you?"

He laughed. "No, but I'm betting my publicist did."

"Thought you needed to impress people even further with your fame?"

"It didn't impress you."

"You don't need to impress me," she responded quickly.

"I know, but it doesn't mean I won't keep trying." He winked and continued toward the elevator, leaving her to ponder the back of his leather jacket.

Did he seriously care? He had millions of women worshipping him, so what was one more? Though considering she still couldn't shake the tremble in her thighs, maybe she was closer to becoming a subject than she allowed herself to believe.

They entered the elevator. The small space brought Valerie right back into the closet. The goose bumps already swarming her skin brought all their friends over for an out-of-control party. Unfortunately, they also invited stomach acid. Alec's question echoed, beckoned.

Do you want me to fuck you?

"Sorry about the suite," he said as they started to ascend.

She straightened her stance and pushed the anxiety down. "It's fine."

Their voices were far too calm. Maybe he was trying to appear nonchalant. She certainly was.

"You seem upset about it." He drew his lips in thoughtfully. "Or something."

Perhaps his composure wasn't an act. His question might not be the only thing on *his* mind.

"I told you it was fine." She clutched her luggage tighter.

Is he seriously okay? Maybe he could just screw her and leave with no consequences. But he hadn't screwed her, because she couldn't say the words. She swallowed, the stomach acid using her esophagus as a waterslide. She couldn't even think the words.

She couldn't tell him she didn't want a stupid cot, and she couldn't say what he needed to hear in the closet. Even with him there telling her he wanted to hear it, she didn't have the confidence to say the words. Besides, she wasn't used to men talking to her like that, and it made her so hot it scared her.

His phone dinged. He took it out and glanced at it. "My mom says hi."

Someone was inside her using her lungs as trampolines. "You just texted your mom?" There was no hiding the shock in her voice.

He smiled his understanding. "Earlier to let her know I got in okay. She's still real big on that, even now."

It had always been Alec and his mom against the world—or more importantly, his father. Even though Alec had escaped him, it still was.

"My mom told me to say hi to you, too."

Were they seriously not going to talk about the closet? If something like that had happened with someone else, she'd be desperate to tell Alec about it, but now...

"Nice cover," he said.

She smirked, relaxed by something familiar to their friendship. Her mom had not told her to say hi to Alec, and she never would have. She thought he was a bad influence because of his father. But Alec wasn't his father. He'd spent his whole life trying to prove that fact.

She considered for the first time that her mother might have been right. Before this weekend, the only thing on Valerie's mind had been receiving the acceptance email from the London Philharmonic, but now Alec had swaggered in, turned her to jelly in a closet, and flipped her mind inside out. No more. She glanced at her phone—still nothing in her inbox.

"Fifth floor," Alec said as the doors opened, "everyone out who doesn't want to *go down*." He licked his lips and waited for her to exit before following her out.

It was a terrible cliché joke, and usually she would have told him so, but now she felt that tongue on her hot skin, that mouth whispering her name.

She exhaled heavily. What had happened in the closet was nothing new to him. He whispered women's names in the dark like he was the announcer at a Bingo game. She needed to get a grip.

Their room was right off the elevator. As soon as they entered, she flicked on every light she could find. Unfortunately that made it so the white and perfectly made bed stared at her from the center of the room.

Her stomach pitched. She couldn't bring herself to say yes to the cot because she didn't want one, but did she want Alec? Did that question even matter anymore?

He seemed over it now—over her now. Of course he was. She wasn't the kind of woman he went for. He was used to models and actresses. It could only have been pity and vodka pulling his strings.

Before she knew what was happening, he stacked his luggage and guitar case in the corner and started stripping. She wanted to ask what he was doing, but she was paused in captivated silence. Her eyes traced the tattoos that spilled along the curves of his shoulders, the strong heft of his arms. His chest and stomach were free of ink, and her eyes continued to invade, slipping past his hard pecs and sliding down his celebrity-fit stomach. She couldn't help counting his ab muscles—one, two, three…

"You going to sleep in your clothes?" he asked with a shrewd smile on his face, his eyes sparkling. He was down to his boxers, and he knew she'd been staring.

God, how long have I been staring?

"What?" she managed.

"Are you sleeping in your clothes?" he repeated slowly, the smile not leaving his lips. It spread wider when he noticed her eyes were still on his stomach—paused at ab muscle number three, to be exact. He slung his jeans over a chair just as his phone rang from the pocket.

Phew. Saved by the bell. *Right?*

"Hey, G." Alec pressed the phone to his ear.

Gideon, Alec's other best friend from high school. It didn't surprise her that they were still close. Alec valued things that were real, true. She knew that came from living with a father who made lies his life goal.

"No fucking way," Alec said.

She tried not to eavesdrop. But she wondered if Alec might

say something about what had happened. If he wouldn't talk to her, he would certainly talk to Gideon. That is, if she made herself scarce. She grabbed her toiletries from her luggage, ducked into the bathroom, and closed the door.

She could hear murmurs as she brushed her teeth. The water was off, her ear to the door, toothpaste foam filling her mouth to an almost choking level so she didn't have to step away. She could only make out certain words: "bed," "peach," "couldn't get," and "so out of your league."

She spit out the toothpaste and cursed under her breath. Gideon had called to talk about his own someone and Alec was not almost-sexing and telling. She wished he wouldn't be a gentleman, just so she could know what to do next.

Should she strip down to her underwear so that she mirrored Alec? Step out of the bathroom in her bra and panties so she wouldn't have to say anything, ask anything? She pressed her ear to the door again, playing with the buttons on her shirt, trying to summon the courage to unbutton them. To be the woman he had awakened.

"Val? She hasn't changed at all."

Alec's words came loud and clear, and the small fire of determination inside her evaporated into smoke.

She hasn't changed at all. She glanced into the mirror, heard the whisper in her mind—*Barking*. If she hadn't changed at all, then that was how he saw her. To Alec she was still dorky, knock-kneed, stringy-hair Valerie. No matter what he said in the closet, no matter how close they came. There it was. He hadn't found her attractive, or even wanted *her*. She was just a body. A place he could stick it.

But wasn't that what he'd told her she needed? *To find someone to fuck.* Not to tell her how beautiful she was, or cuddle with her after, or marry her, but fuck.

Even with his question still unanswered, it shouldn't be Alec. She clearly couldn't handle it.

She stepped out of the bathroom. Alec was off the phone and in bed, the covers to his waist. His tattooed skin against the white sheets was dizzying.

"I sleep naked," he said, his eyes an even deeper brown.

Her pulse sped like an out-of-control metronome. *He's naked under there?*

Of course he was. As if the bed wasn't enough, as if his sculpted chest wasn't enough, she had to deal with the hardness that had been teasing her in the closet, bare against those pristine sheets.

"Not tonight, though?" she asked, hoping to hide the shakiness in her voice.

He pulled the sheets back to reveal his plaid boxers and laughed. "No," he acquiesced, "not tonight."

"Hilarious," she said, expelling a grateful sigh. She headed over to her suitcase to grab her pajamas, a robin egg blue tank top and boy shorts, and went back to the bathroom to change.

She was just about to close the door when Alec clicked off the light. "But who knows about tomorrow night?"

Chapter Four

Light trickled into the hotel room and dappled Alec and Valerie in shared sunshine. His morning wood—he glanced over at Val's back rising and falling under the covers—was caused by a lot more than the morning.

Why hadn't he finished what they'd started last night?

Because it wasn't only his decision.

The minute they'd been interrupted by Randy, Valerie started acting like a terrified animal. Like he was a fox and she was a hare and she had no intention of getting near his mouth, or more specifically the cock straining against his boxers, ever again.

Though he was disappointed, he understood. Anxieties had churned through his mind, too. The loudest being, *what would the morning after be like?*

Their morning after was now, sunlight continuing to creep around the sides of the drapes and Val at the farthest edge of their bed.

If she was afraid to touch him by mistake as they slept, if she couldn't talk to him last night, if his usual jokes were coming off like innuendo—and fine, maybe they *were*—what he'd wanted so singularly in the closet could never happen. Their friendship couldn't take it and shouldn't have to. Their friendship had withstood a lot over the years, had been the glue that held him together when his father broke him over and over again.

Sober and in the morning light with no body parts confusing them—well, other than his currently hard cock—last night seemed like a terrible mistake.

Logically, he knew this, but he couldn't stop thinking how she turned to liquid below the sweep of his lips, his fingers. He couldn't help replaying her moan over and over. Just thinking of it drowned him in warm shivers, the kind that could only be soothed by hearing it again.

His cock grew even harder. Fuck, he needed to let this go.

He slunk out of bed to use the bathroom and when he returned, Valerie was awake, sitting up against the pillow.

"You snore," she said.

"I've always snored."

"I know. I guess I forgot." She stretched, and her breasts pulled against the light blue fabric of her tank top.

He tried to look away from her, but he couldn't. The sunlight was casting glitter in her rumpled hair, a glow on her cheeks. Seeing her glimmering in early morning sunlight brought a memory, too, whisked him back to all the times he'd slept at her house in high school—the smell of pancakes or coffee wafting up from her kitchen. The smell of a normal family, something he didn't have.

The heady aroma was as much the reason he stayed over as Val being his best friend. He never got to partake, though. The smell of breakfast was his cue to go. If her parents ever found him in her room, they'd distrust him even more than they did already. Alec had been Val's one rebellion.

He stole a glance at her nipples stabbing through cotton.

How could he help wanting to be her rebellion again?

"You sleep okay otherwise?" He wondered if he should get back into the bed. They weren't in her high school bedroom anymore. He didn't have to sneak out at the first slant of light against the sheets.

"Sure, fine." She ran her hands through her hair.

He was frozen, unsure what to say or what to do. Fuck. He had to bring up last night. He had to do something. Avoiding the subject would make for a weekend full of this—uncomfortable niceties and silences. So not them.

Maybe she'd agree it had been a mistake and they could chalk last night up to nostalgia and too much vodka. They hadn't gone so far that they couldn't take it all back yet. They could just return to the way things were. For their friendship, logic would have to win out.

He returned to bed and took a deep, centering breath. He was about to speak when Val talked first.

"Yes," she spoke into the air in front of her. "I've had time to think about it, and the answer to your question is yes."

He sat up, echoed her stance. The two of them filled the mirror across from the bed, their backs tight against the headboard, messy haired, sleep worn.

Yes?
Yes.
Yes!
NO!

His cock battered against his boxers, but this was a bad idea. Just because he didn't want anyone else to fuck her didn't mean he should. Unfortunately, the current radio station he'd managed to tune his brain to didn't change that she'd been all he thought about since their bodies were startled apart by Randy Tines.

"Are you going to say anything?" she asked.

Of course, he wanted her, but was that enough?

"You couldn't have said that last night?" Better to keep his response light. As if he could take it or leave it. Even though, who was he kidding?

Not his still-hard cock, that was for sure.

She glanced at him sideways. "I could always change my answer." She'd never put up with his shit, and it was clear she wasn't about to start now.

"But I'll always know you said yes to begin with," he replied, still not moving.

Why was he hesitating? He was in bed next to a hot woman who wanted to fuck him right now. Instead of fulfilling her fantasy, he was wavering his way out of where he'd been desperate to be last night—inside her hungry, wet pussy.

Man up, Alec. Best friend or not, she is telling you to fuck her.

No more talking, no more thinking. He'd fuck her so hard she'd shriek the answer he'd waited for like it was the only word she knew. She'd forever equate the affirmative with the plunge of his cock. He reached for her. His fingers were inches away from those teasing nipples when she pulled back.

"I have rules."

"What?" His voice was filled with shocked laughter. He pressed his outstretched hands against the bed. He should have known it wouldn't be so easy.

"If we're going to do this," she said, her face so serious he thought it might crack, "there are things we need—"

"I have rules, too," he interrupted. He didn't at the moment, but Val's maturity always did that to him. It was something he admired and tried, though usually failed, to copy.

"Mine first." She focused her eyes on the mirror across the room and away from him. "I want an orgasm."

He couldn't help but laugh again, a sputtered spit laugh, not at her but at her bluntness.

She glared at him, her cheeks pricked pink. She clearly didn't see the joke, but hell, that request was too fun not to play with her a little bit.

"Just one?" he retorted.

"Please." She sighed, staring down at her hands. "If you're okay with it, say *agree*."

"Okay," he said, putting the brakes on his laughter. "Agree." He would give her an orgasm. He would give her twenty orgasms. He was always an overachiever when it came to her.

"Rule number two." She opened her hand and ticked off a finger. "While we're doing it you need to treat me like one of the women you sleep with."

"Fuck, you mean."

"Excuse me?"

"Like the women I fuck." He spoke slowly, letting the words hit her like hot raindrops.

"Right," she replied, the blush in her cheeks running down her neck and washing over her bare shoulders.

He splayed his fingers out on the mattress. "If we're going to do this, Val, you can say the word. Actually, you have to — that's one of my rules."

"Fine." She sighed again. "I want you to treat me like one of the women you fuck."

"Agree." The sound of that word on her lips would make him agree to just about anything. His cock rising even higher was his solemn swear.

"Wait, are you 'fucking' anyone right now?" The skin on her face blistered with concern.

"No, not at this very moment." He intensified his gaze, hoping he was illustrating just how much he'd like to be.

"When was the last time you had sex?"

"Sex, sex?" He leaned back on the pillow. "Or sexual contact?"

"Don't make me feel like an idiot for asking, especially when you answer questions that way."

"Stop slut shaming me," he said with mock irritation. "There's nothing wrong with consensual sex between two adults. That's what you're asking for, isn't it?"

Her breath was measured. "All I'm getting at is that when this is happening between us, I want to be the only one. It's not like you tell me about every woman you're with."

"That sounds like you're asking to be a lot more than just a woman I'm fucking," he replied with a sweeping gaze, even though she was right. He didn't tell her about every woman he was with, because most of them didn't last long enough to even bother.

"Stop being an asshole."

"Calm down, Val, I haven't slept with anyone in two weeks."

"Two weeks?" She whistled. "Going for a record?"

"Now who's being an asshole?"

There was a threatening gleam in her eyes. "Maybe we should just forget this whole thing."

He huffed. "I can't believe you think I would hurt you like that. You're my friend."

She shook her head. "You're already breaking rule number two. When we're fucking"—the word came out like a foreign language on her lips—"I'm not your friend."

"Understood." He fought a smile. This was a whole lot to remember while he was required to rock her world.

"You need to promise me, though. You can't be involved with anyone else, not even one of your little groupies."

"Agreed. Do you need me to put my hand on the bible in the nightstand?" His response was flippant, though he knew why she needed him to repeat it. He'd never hidden his reputation from her. She had a right to be worried if she really was about to be a woman he was fucking.

His eyes feasted on the slope of Val's neck and lower, settling on the provocative line between the fabric and the curve of her tits. He couldn't wait until she was a woman he was fucking.

"No talking about how we feel," she continued.

"You're telling *me* you want it to be only about sex."

"Oh right, I forgot I was talking to Cock-fucius," she replied, a smile finally creeping out. "No kissing."

He folded his arms over his chest. "I think you've seen *Pretty Woman* too many times."

"Considering you know that, how many times have you seen it, tough guy?"

"What? Hooker Julia Roberts is a babe," he said as cover.

She rolled her eyes. "She's also smart. Kissing is far too intimate."

He ran his hand beside where her thigh lay under the blankets. He didn't touch her, but was close enough he could have. "Even without kissing, it's going to get intimate."

She fought a smile but stayed silent. He needed to get her through these rules soon or he was going to explode.

"Agree," he said. They hadn't kissed last night, and it had been hot as hell. No kissing was fine by him. "Wait, you mean on the lips only, right?"

She didn't respond, just ticked off another finger. "You can't tell anyone. Not even Gideon."

"I would never talk to Gideon about this."

"I heard my name last night."

"Were you eavesdropping?"

She ignored him and continued. "We only do this once." She ticked off another finger.

"Seriously, should I get a pen?"

"No, that's the last one, but it's the most important."

"Only once?" he repeated. Of course once was better than never. But once meant if they did this now, they had two more days together to deal with the aftermath, and more importantly to try and not do it again.

"You need to say agree," she pressed.

"Whatever you want." He flipped up his hands. "I'm doing this for you."

A knowing tease snarled her lips. "That wasn't how it felt last night."

"Agree," he coughed out. Better than admit that, fuck, he wanted this, too. He more than wanted it.

"Okay." She nodded. "I think we're all set."

"Finally," he said. Oh hell, was he ready. He snaked his hand into the space between them and set his sights on the swollen bud of her nipple. The need inside him deepened with each impending inch…

"No." She slapped his hand down. "Shower first."

He looked from his denied hand to her face. He'd played her game long enough. It was time to take control. He grabbed her wrist, demanding her attention. "Speaking to you like a woman I'm fucking," he said, straddling her at the waist so she was pinned against the bed. "There is no fucking way you are getting in that shower yet."

She didn't protest, didn't do anything but emit a delicious sigh as his cock pressed into her leg.

"We didn't go over my rules." He ground his hips against hers, sheets that smelled of them the only barrier. "And the most important one is that I get to figure out what you like first." He punctuated each word with a pound of his hard cock against the soft inside of her thigh. "So I can be sure the orgasm you're demanding is definite when I do finally fuck you."

Her eyes blazed below him. She swallowed, her lips parted. He continued to grind, and the room spun. He lifted up just enough to pull away the sheets and straddled her again, the hot skin of her upper thighs singeing his own. He ran his hands over her tits, the pearls of her nipples, slowly, his fingertips sliding like oil.

"Agree?" he asked.

"Agree," she whispered.

"How's this?" He indicated the slow trickle of his fingers over her nipples.

"Not bad."

"Truthful," he admitted. "You might not be able to answer the next time I ask you." He touched his mouth to them. His hands pressed into the bed as his lips traced the arch of her tits, feather-soft above the fabric of her tank top. He breathed hot desire onto her nipples, and they responded, seemed to reach for his hidden tongue. His gut exploded with need. But he didn't rip her shirt off and suck at her like he was desperate to—he teased. Showing her what she had really gotten herself into.

This was not going to be a *wham bam thank you sir*. Oh no, she was going to have to deal with wanting him so badly she forgot her name.

"Take your shirt off," he instructed.

She stared at him defiantly.

"Take your fucking shirt off and show me what I signed on for."

She didn't flinch. "But I'm not wearing a bra."

"Why do you think I want it off?" he replied, his tongue grazing her ear.

She didn't lose his gaze as she removed it, though she was doing her best to keep her shivers in check as he inspected her.

"Those are some great fucking tits," he said. "I can't wait until they're putty in my hands while you ride my cock."

Her eyes widened.

It was what he would have said to a woman he was fucking, but the minute he saw her full B's, creamy as vanilla ice cream, with perky little nipples like cherries on top, taut and tight and waiting for him, he couldn't help picturing just that. Valerie on top of him on this bed, taking him deep, her hands clutching the headboard as he slid inside her again and again.

"Thanks, I grew them myself," she joked.

He smiled, but not in amusement. "Just thought of another rule. You need to treat me like a guy you're just fucking. Would you say that to a guy you're just fucking?"

Her breath caught. "I've never just fucked anyone."

He knew it was true, knew why this decision had been so hard for both of them to come to, but he wasn't about to get caught up in that, now that he was so close.

"Tell me to suck on them."

Her eyes were hooded.

"You want me to, right?" He pressed into her soft flesh, and her head lolled back in a gasp. His heartbeat hammered in time with his cock. Fuck, the way her body responded was sexy. It knew him as well as she did—each breath, each whimper exactly what he needed to hear.

She nodded. Her tongue darted out to wet her lips.

"You wanted it last night, too, didn't you? Wanted me to take your nipple into my mouth, circle my tongue around it slowly, and squeeze it between my lips. Give you a preview of what I'd do when I went to work on your clit."

Her mouth opened, but nothing came, no words, no breath. Though he knew she was locked not in fear but desire.

Greedy lust shot into his cock. He had her. "That's the best part about just fucking someone. You can tell him exactly what you want. So what do you want?"

...

Valerie's mind sparked like an engine that had been jumped.

Tell him what she wanted. The only word she could focus on in that moment was *more*. Showing her exactly what he would do as his lips and tongue made their way down her body. Down to the place that was wet and waiting for him, again.

He was her best friend; she could tell him. "Not my breasts," she managed. "Lower." Her pulse battered in her ears as she waited for his response.

She tried to forget she was practically naked in front of him. That he was seeing her body, seeing all of her. She pushed away her usual insecurities.

Alec's head cocked. "You want me working that clit already?"

That was exactly what she wanted, but she was glad he was saying it so she didn't have to. She nodded, afraid if she said yes, it would come out like a scream. She'd never wanted anything more in her life.

He slid down the length of her body and lapped at her stomach, flicking his tongue along the waistband of her boy shorts, lathing it over her belly button, teasing like it was his only purpose in life.

"Should I keep going?" His breath sizzled against her abdomen.

She stared at the top of his sleep-scuffed head, the carved muscles of his back as he continued to torment her with his mouth. His lips explored from one side of her to the other, the heat of his gasps building like her need. Her body was so ready for him to go lower. Her want was like a color she could see. He dragged his tongue along her waistline again, gearing up to undo her. That is, if she could ask for it.

"I could taste your stomach all day, Dirty Girl, but I don't think that's what you want, is it?"

She shook her head.

"You want me to taste you, don't you? You want me to rip your panties off and fuck you with my tongue, don't you?

Suck on that clit of yours like it's a lollipop."

"Yes," she breathed. "Fuck." The word tumbled out. "Yes."

"Now we're talking, Dirty Girl." He grabbed her ass and pulled her to him. "Take your shorts off, but leave the panties on."

She had no idea her hands could move that fast. In seconds, her shorts were on the floor with her discarded tank top.

His eyes went dark, possessive. "Look at you, breathing wild and half naked waiting for me to make you come."

She felt those words all the way down to her toes. Why had no one ever talked to her like this? Why had she never known how much she would like it?

He angled his mouth against the dripping lace fabric of her panties. "You'll get what you want." His voice rumbled against the wet warmth of her. "But you're not ready yet. I want you so soaked and swollen that the minute my tongue touches your begging clit, you explode in my mouth."

He was getting her there. He breathed against her as he rubbed two fingers at the fabric right above... *Oh my God*, it felt so good she couldn't help but buck against him.

"Harder, Dirty Girl? You want it harder?"

She opened her mouth but she couldn't form words; all that came out was a low moan.

"Of course you do, you don't have to answer. Your body is begging me for it."

She considered asking him to fuck her. Hard, now, the headboard smacking against the top of her head, but the teasing delighted her. Having a man do exactly what she wanted him to wasn't something she was going to waste.

His fingers went at her relentlessly, hitting a rhythm like she was a guitar and he was playing the most exquisite solo. She was going to lose her mind if she wasn't in his mouth soon. It was so close, panting pure want into her core.

"Lick me." The words hung in the air for a moment until she realized she'd said them.

Alec glanced up at her, his expression teeming with want, his lips full and ready to take her. "Don't like being kept waiting, Dirty Girl?"

She was breathing so hard she hiccupped, but nothing inside her body was attached anymore. Alec's words were a sledgehammer splintering her organs and sending them flying off into the deepest reaches of desire.

He ran one finger down the length of her thigh. "Say that again while I can see your face, and I'll obey."

A burning bloomed in her stomach. "Lick me," she repeated.

His eyes sparked deep brown, turning almost red. "Time to take care of rule number one." He slipped her underwear to the side. "I'll save the unveiling until I get to be inside you." His breath was white-hot against the steam of her and, when his tongue made contact with her throbbing center, her whole body coiled, contracted. *Oh God,* she was going to orgasm from just one flick of his tongue. The foreplay of last night and this morning converged and began to untwist the knot at her core.

"You're about to come for me, aren't you, Dirty Girl?"

About to? No, she was, the rush overflowing as he slid two fingers inside her and continued to lavish her with his tongue. Liquid pleasure assaulted Valerie's every sense, streaking in luscious, fiery waves over her skin. She bucked against him, her insides contracting in pings of electric shock, doused by sweet release. Alec sucked at her, lapping up every last gasp.

He sat up, his lips shiny with her, the tattoos on his shoulders beating as hard as his heart must have been. "*Now* I'll shower."

"You don't have to. We can…" she started. Even though she had just been satisfied, her only thought became *put what*

I felt against my thigh inside me now. But she couldn't say it. He'd given her permission. He'd demanded it. But without his hands on her, without his mouth on her, she didn't have the courage to ask.

"You want another orgasm already? Don't be greedy. I haven't even had one yet."

Before she could respond, Alec rose from the bed, stepped into the bathroom, and closed the door. She heard him brushing his teeth. A minute later, the shower turned on. Should she join him in there?

She fisted the sheets. If she'd told him they weren't allowed to kiss because of the intimacy, showering together was out of the question.

She could already feel the trickle of hot water running over her head, the way Alec's chest would harden under her hands as she slicked him with soap, how he would pin her into the corner and ease inside her, the marble tile cold against her back. Aside from the intimacy, that would also mean he would see her naked, standing in the bright light of the bathroom. The same bathroom that held the mirror that had made her terrible nickname repeat in her mind last night.

Even if she could gather the courage, she didn't think she could stand. He'd melted her from the inside out. Her bones were white lava. And she still had actually having sex with him to look forward to.

She needed to let people just fuck her more often.

Chapter Five

"You better tell me what the hell is going on," Cynthia screeched, her blue eyes dancing.

Valerie sat with her at one of the twenty picnic tables set up on the grounds of the hotel, next to what looked like the makings of a track meet. Reece Freedland yelled over a megaphone at the front of the festivities, her blond hair in a tight braid and a whistle around her neck.

Valerie and Alec had already gotten the eye from Reece for missing breakfast. They'd gone for tongue service and room service instead, and she didn't think talking during the rundown of the rest of the day's activities—lawn games, a barbecue lunch, cocktails, and late night mini golf—was going to be tolerated.

Were they at a reunion, on a cruise, or in hell?

She'd thought the way Reece used to treat her in high school might fill her with enough remorse to leave her alone, but maybe only Valerie remembered the taunts. Maybe like she should have been able to, Reece had moved on.

"Nothing," Valerie said out of the side of her mouth,

ironically using the skills she'd learned in high school for talking while under the scrutiny of a boring authoritarian to respond to Cynthia.

Her eyes squinted in disbelief. "It didn't look like nothing last night. It didn't sound like it, either." She giggled.

Valerie remembered the noises, the words Alec brought out of her just that morning, and her skin boiled.

"It's that or we talk about who got fat. Your gossip is way more fun," Cynthia pressed, leaning toward Valerie.

Valerie wondered if people were gossiping about her and Alec. How they may have belonged together in high school, but they were not even close to being equals now. *Barking* didn't belong with beautiful.

"We're just friends," she said, even as she recalled the rip of his two fingers slicing into her, the complete hypnosis of his tongue.

"You've been saying that for years," Cynthia dismissed with a wave.

Unlike with Alec, Valerie hadn't spoken to Cynthia very much at all since high school. They'd kept in touch a bit through college, they were friends on Facebook, but she didn't have actual proof that Valerie *had* been saying that for years. Even though, of course, it was true.

In high school she'd said it to the other people in band, in college to her junior-year roommate, up until a few months ago to Charles whenever he got jealous of their late night phone calls. She understood now how *just friends* sounded like a lie.

She repeated *just friends* in her mind as she glanced over and found Alec whispering to a guy at the table next to them. Who would Alec have been talking to so familiarly? She studied him, the broad heft of his shoulders under a polo shirt, angular features punctuated by tortoise-shell frames. Oh—Gideon.

Holy crap, is that Gideon?

Like Alec, the years had been good to him. It was like the two of them had been dough in high school and now they were hard, golden, delicious sugar cookies fresh from the oven.

She stole another glance at Alec. He'd showered but hadn't shaved, stubble dusting his jaw and shadowing the curve of his lips. Her mouth watered. *Just friends*, she repeated, even though all she wanted in that moment was to take a huge, mouth-filling bite.

It was what she should have repeated in her head this morning, instead of allowing him to sexually short-circuit her and replace that safe barrier with one word: "more."

"You're seriously not going to tell me?" Cynthia pulled at the hem of her tomato-red T-shirt.

What are he and Gideon whispering about? Hopefully he was keeping the secret that Cynthia was working on getting out of her.

God, did she want to admit it. Maybe it would take some of the taboo away. It might be smart to do something to make it less illicit, less hot, because if she didn't, she was never going to be able to follow her own rules.

If she didn't say the words but just nodded, would that be okay?

Besides, she was desperate for someone to know. Just look at him. She still was, the way his tattoos turned oil black in the sun and his mouth was swollen from her. She couldn't stop.

"Listen, I'm divorced," Cynthia tried again. "I haven't had sex"—she lingered on the word—"in almost a year. Give me something."

"I'm not allowed to talk about it."

Cynthia slapped the table, bringing a look of rage from Reece. "Which means," she whispered when Reece's eyes moved on, "there is something to talk about."

Val nodded, thousands of tiny sparks tingling in her abdomen.

"Oh my God," Cynthia said, "I knew it. I knew it before

we got here."

Valerie shook her head.

"Nothing before we got here?" She stuck a manicured finger to her lips.

Valerie shook her head harder.

"Whatever, just keep telling yourself that." She threw her hands up. "Your foreplay has lasted fourteen years."

Those words hit Valerie in the gut, the sparks in her stomach doused in ice water. *Has it?* Because that would mean she'd wanted this for a very long time. It wasn't like she had a date stamp on their relationship. *Before Fucking*, she thought, smiling at the words in her head, and *After Fucking*. Like Alec was her sexual messiah.

No, she felt exactly how she'd always felt about Alec. The only difference now was that she wanted him to feel her, all over, everywhere. Wanted him to do what he'd done that morning again and again and again. She wanted everyone here but the two of them to disappear so he could take her on one of these picnic tables. Screw the splinters…

Cynthia snapped her fingers. "Hey, all that stuff you're reliving, you better remember that I'm getting it out of you at some point this weekend."

Val smiled. She knew that regardless of her rule, Cynthia probably would.

She knocked her knee against Val's under the table. "I can't believe it. It must have been amazing. Just look at him."

And Val did yet again, the heft of his shoulders accentuated by a tight black T-shirt. The exchange between her and Cynthia was so familiar. It was like they were back in the cafeteria, and Alec was a guy she had a crush on.

But this was Alec. She couldn't have a crush on him. At least *Before Fucking* Valerie couldn't.

"So," Cynthia gushed, "are you guys together now?"

Val shook her head.

Cynthia's face twisted in confusion. "You two have always been your own thing."

She supposed that was true, but Cynthia didn't know the whole story. Valerie had never told her about the day Alec tried to turn their friendship into everything. The day after graduation, he'd come to her house with his life strapped to his back asking her to gamble on his future, what he said could be their future, rather than go after her own.

She wanted to be able to say yes, but she knew back then that Alec couldn't be her savior when he still needed one so badly. He'd played off her rejection that day, but they hadn't spoken for almost two years. It took almost five more to repair what had broken, to get their friendship back on solid ground, and now they were playing roulette yet again.

"Here," Cynthia said, reaching into her pocket and sliding something shiny across the table.

"A condom?" Val shout-whispered, hiding it in her pocket before anyone could see.

"I brought a bunch of them. After last night I thought you might need one."

Val hadn't even thought of it. She definitely hadn't brought some. In all her rules that morning, she hadn't even talked to Alec about safe sex. Of course, if she knew him like she did, he'd brought a bunch of them, too.

"Thanks," Val said, even as uncertainty boomed and cracked through her. She and Alec were going to have sex.

She and Alec were going to *have sex*.

"Oh my God." Cynthia put her hand to her mouth and whispered between her fingers, "He's coming over here."

"Don't say anything," Val scolded, once again remembering this same scene played out inside the walls of their high school.

Back then, Alec had even been there sometimes sitting next to Cynthia in silence, his coffee brown eyes watching

Valerie as the boy she liked hit their cafeteria table. But now he stood above them in a tight black T-shirt and tighter black jeans, a studded belt around his waist, his tattoos shadows in the sun—a rock star at a picnic.

"You want to be on my team for this crap?" The same eyes that had watched her orgasm into his mouth that morning were on her now.

"Team?" Val asked.

"For the obstacle course. You guys haven't been listening, have you?" A roguish sneer flashed on his lips.

"No, we were listening." Cynthia spoke fast. "She just felt bad because I don't have a partner. But I'm not participating anyway. I have a bad…" She paused, her save almost perfect. "Foot," she finished, wearing a cantaloupe slice of a smile.

"Sure, I'll be on your team." The words came out breathy. Not at all in the casual way they should have when she responded to Alec about such a simple question.

"Okay," he drawled like he'd noted it, too, "let's get set up, then."

She rose and walked with him to where the other teams were waiting. A potato sack lay on the ground in front of them. Their paired-off classmates gathered in front of their own potato sacks. She glanced down the line and saw Gideon on a team with Georgia Cahill—past head cheerleader, always jerk—the girl leader of the group who'd called her *Barking*.

Was she thinking that word now?

Her blond hair was up in a high ponytail. She wore napkin-sized white shorts and a red halter top, her body all tan and curves. Gideon's looks had caught up to hers, that was for sure, but what the hell were they doing on the same team?

Why did she care? She had her own awkward pairing to worry about.

Gideon noticed her, smiled, and waved.

She responded in kind, but something about his smile, the

way it curled up on only one side, made it seem like he knew something. The same thing Cynthia now knew.

"You didn't tell him, did you?" Valerie had no right to ask, but standing in silence seemed worse.

"What, and break one of your rules?" he whispered into her ear. "No, Dirty Girl, I kept my mouth shut about your fabulous pussy."

She swallowed a blistering breath. Apparently that nickname was sticking, as were his abdomen-twisting words. She would have told him to stop, if she could get her lips to move. But something about the way he spoke, about being known that way to someone, sent prickles of steamy electricity between her trembling legs.

"What about you—you and Cynthia get up to your old tricks?"

"No," she replied quickly, "I didn't say anything." She hadn't, not literally anyway.

"Gideon has his own stuff going on."

Valerie leaned in closer. "Does it involve Georgia?"

"Secrets are secrets for a reason," he said, laying his pointer finger on her lips.

That finger. She remembered where it had been earlier, where she couldn't wait for it to be again. He pulled it away, put his hands in his back pockets.

"You have secrets, too." His eyes roamed over her face. He was so much taller now that she had sneakers on instead of her heels. If he pulled her into an embrace, her head would hit right at the center of his chest, that mouthwateringly taut chest. She never would have thought of it *B.F.* but now their closeness made her want more closeness, made her crave it like an addict.

She forced herself to look away. God did she ever have secrets. Number one was that she'd never come close to experiencing anything like what had happened between them, and Cock-fucius help her, she couldn't wait for it to happen again.

Chapter Six

Alec was not a sportsman, and even after brushing his teeth and a shower, he could still sense Valerie all over him. Having her near him now was not helping his game. She was attached to him, literally—by rope at the ankles and the edge of his torso by his arm as they ran toward the next obstacle. His goal was supposed to be hitting that far-off cone, but as her curves banked tight against him, his only aim was getting through this fucking maze so he could touch her again, taste her again.

Reece seemed to be using anything she could think of to keep them busy, like they were children who would misbehave if they weren't given something to occupy them at every moment—idle hands, and all that.

Maybe she was right. Look where the activity his classmates had come up with last night had brought him. To Valerie riding his mouth like it was a mechanical bull, her legs spread wide while she filled him with her musky juice, while she begged for it. Fuck, if they were alone right now…

But they weren't. The whole group of his classmates littered the lawn behind the hotel in potato sacks, or attached like he and Valerie were, or preparing for a tug-of-war. All of them seemed, at least for the moment, even younger than they had in high school.

There had been the initial rush of attention when he arrived that morning, hugs and back slaps and selfies. People who didn't even know he existed in high school fawning about how much they loved his music. He was used to the swarms; they happened a lot. And he'd expected this one.

What he hadn't expected was Val standing next to him giving the people who gave him crap in high school—for wearing the same clothes he wore the day before, or being wrapped in a jacket on the hottest of days—crap right back.

"Amazing how fame makes a person worth your time," she said to a group of giggling women who'd been on the cheerleading squad as they each took their turn giving him a too-long hug. "At least he has a name tag on so you don't have to ask," she added when the crowd kept squeezing without pause.

They might have been able to brush off Valerie's outburst, but he heard her loud and clear. Her words weren't jealous, they were protective. She was his best friend and these women were fake bitches and she wanted them to know it.

"What's with Val?" one of them had asked.

"She's my bodyguard," was all he could think to reply.

He'd always wanted to be the one who shielded her, but she was so much stronger than he was. He supposed that came from not having a father who'd convinced you that you were shit every day of your life. Alec could remember wishing his father had been an alcoholic so he could blame the way he'd treated him on something. As it was, Alec only had himself to blame.

"You didn't have to say that," he said when the cheerleaders had left.

"I might not have had the courage to in high school, but there is no way I'm letting that shit go now."

His eyebrows shot up.

"What? You shouldn't, either."

He knew she was right, but the part of him that was still that same scared boy wanted the attention of those women. Even if they didn't deserve it, he needed to know that he did. It was the only thing that kept him going most days, kept the echoes of his father's words quiet. *Look how many people love me. Look how many people think I am special.*

He wondered how much longer he would carry that little boy around. At twenty-nine he was getting exceptionally heavy.

Valerie's arm pinched at his side, reminding him they were currently participating in the damn obstacle course. He couldn't believe he'd agreed. He was not a rule follower. But he needed distraction. He actually needed Reece's stupid activities.

If he and Valerie had stayed in the room, they would have fucked. The one time she'd mandated finished and over hour one. If sex between them was only happening once, he wanted to savor it. Build the need he already felt. Crave the taste of her a little longer.

He tried to concentrate on the race, but all he could think of as the rope burned the skin of his ankle was tightening that same rope around Valerie's wrists, pulling her taut to that headboard, so he could use his tongue to make her even crazier than he had that morning. Or maybe if she really was the dirty girl he thought she was, she'd tie him up.

Her brown hair was up in a ponytail, a bright pink tank top and black shorts over her adorable little ass. A white bra strap slanted over one shoulder like a finger, beckoning.

He'd given a lot of women orgasms over the years, but he'd never quite delighted in it as much as he had with Valerie. He wanted her to feel good because she was his friend, and because her body demanded to be worshipped. Not just the outside of her, either. Not just her skin like hot white sugar, her tits perky and the perfect handful, her smooth stomach, and her pussy. There was something inside her, too, that he'd never realized until he'd started to release it—a flame on low that his attention had turned to a raging blaze—that kept him close and humming like a moth now.

He needed to stop, to remember where they were. What they were doing. His pants were way too tight. If the boner that threatened to rip got to full mast, his entire high school graduating class would see it.

"Hurry up," Val directed, waking him from his fantasy. "Faster," she insisted, sparking a new one. *Faster* falling from her lips as his cock entered her again and again and again. He had an idea of how it would feel. His tongue and fingers remembering she was tight, wet, and as quick to respond as a servant… Stop—he had to make himself stop.

"I'm going as fast as I can." He wobbled along with her. "You seriously care about winning this thing?"

"If I play," she huffed, "I win."

Typical Val; he always admired her confident spirit and belief that she deserved to win. He'd never thought that about himself, even with all he had accomplished.

Why was he still carrying that little boy? He was a famous rock star, for fuck's sake. His father didn't have the power to tamp out his destiny any more. But, being with all these people, being in this town, was bringing the tyrannical thumb of his father right back, choking his larynx. The first time his father hit him was the last time Alec believed that love didn't come with consequences. That being hurt was the rule, not the exception.

"Alec," Valerie demanded, pulling at his ankle with her own, "wake up."

"It's just a dumb ribbon. I can buy you one."

"For what?"

He had some ideas. Maybe *Best Woman I Ever Tasted*. "Whatever, whatever you want to win for. I'll buy you a room of them if we can run a little slower."

"Awww," she played, not letting up on her pace, "is Al out

of shape, too many late nights partying?"

"I'm not out of shape," he said, moving faster, "this is just stupid." He'd show her how fucking in shape he was when he finally made her come around his cock.

"Then why did you ask to be my partner?"

He didn't answer, even though it was completely clear to him. He might have been avoiding going back to the room, but he also knew to keep his sanity he had to prove he could be near her without losing his fucking mind. He was trying to get himself to remember *this* was them. Not what had happened in the room, even though he couldn't stop thinking about going back there.

They finally reached the next cone, removed the rope, and moved on to the next obstacle—crawling through a set of tubes made out of tent material.

He glanced down at his pants. "I am not dressed for this." Like everything he owned, his outfit was tight, black, and studded. Clothes made for playing guitar, not playing catch.

"Who packed for you, Marilyn Manson?"

"My stylist," he admitted. He let him do everything when it came to clothes. Alec was too lazy, too busy to care what he wore.

She rolled her eyes. "Even worse."

He pulled on the legs of his jeans. "I really can't bend down in these."

She shrugged dismissively. "Then take them off." It was a joke Val would have made hundreds of times before this weekend, but now it froze them. Her cheeks bloomed, her lips pressed together.

He moved closer to her, unable to fight it anymore. "I only do that for dirty girls," he whispered. "You know any?"

"We have four more obstacles left," she breathed. Her eyes became all pupils, and he knew he had her.

"You must want that ribbon real bad." He slid his finger

along her bra strap. Her skin was damp with sweat, her heavy breaths going uneven as he continued to play with the satiny fabric. "More than you want anything."

"I wouldn't say that." Her bottom lip caught between her teeth.

They were locked in place, the world still moving around them.

"What trumps the ribbon?" He forced himself to let go of her bra strap so he didn't rip it off of her.

"I think you saw that this morning."

His abdomen gnashed and roared. Oh, fuck had he ever.

"Besides," she continued, "if we're only going to be together once, I figure we shouldn't rush that."

"Definitely not." It was the same thought he'd had, but that thought was falling fast.

A line was forming behind them. People were waiting to get into the next obstacle instead of cutting in front of them. They were watching. He was famous now, and even though they couldn't hear their conversation, they wanted to see what was going to happen.

He did, too.

"But," she finally said, "it's not like we have to wait or anything. That's not a rule."

He waved his arm at the gathering crowd. "Go around," he said, grabbing Val at the waist and guiding her out of the way. "We both have cramps," he declared, thinking fast.

"I always knew you two were on the same cycle," Brandon White, ex–high school quarterback, current NFL one, panted, pushing past them. His partner was another ex–football player who didn't play for an NFL team, and his flabby body showed it.

You'd think the astronomical probability that two famous people had come from the same graduating class would link them somehow, but clearly Brandon wasn't into commiserating on their lottery-level odds. Alec didn't even bother to respond. At least he had a hot woman as his partner.

At least he had a hot woman he was about to fuck.

"We would have beaten you if we didn't stop," Val yelled to the bottom of Brandon's shoes as he slugged through the obstacle. "Once a douchebag, always a douchebag." She shook her head.

"People don't change."

"You have."

Outside, there was no doubt he had, but inside he wasn't any different. He was still the guy who chose avoidance over pain. But she wasn't asking for what was inside him, she wanted his body, and that he could give her.

Her lips trembled, waiting for his response. He wanted to kiss her, but that was a rule. There were also people around, and that was another. He was surprised he was keeping them all straight because thinking of Val like this, seeing her like this, was making everything hazy, in a good way.

The foghorn whistle announced the end of the race. The winners jumped up and down, hooted and slapped five.

"Guess I'm buying you that room full of ribbons."

She staked her hand on top of his. "I don't want anything I don't work for."

All their words were innuendo now; all their movements were foreplay. He was going to make her work. That was for sure.

"You're okay with not staying for lunch?" As much as he wanted her, he wanted to be wanted by her even more.

"If you're hungry, we could get room service again," she suggested, one eyebrow up.

"I'm not hungry."

She ran a finger along the length of his cheek, innocent enough, but with everything that was between them she might as well have been stroking his cock with warm lube. "I am."

He moved her hand to his belt buckle. "Let's get you fed."

Chapter Seven

Once the elevator doors closed and they were finally alone, he couldn't wait anymore. He circled his arms around her waist and pressed his chest into the soft contours of her tits. He drove his cock against her leg feverishly, losing himself in the ache.

His lips were desperate to go for hers. His need for them was almost stronger than the need pulsing through his cock, but he kissed her jaw instead. Lay hot, furious kisses all along the angle of her chin and into the soft skin at the tip of her neck.

He cornered her against the wall. He couldn't move his hands fast enough, his lips fast enough, his cock threatened to rip through his five-hundred-dollar jeans, but everything became this moment. Their two bodies searching desperately for any contact, any release—each other.

"Reece is going to kill us." Val laughed.

"Fuck Reece." Alec slid his tongue along her neck and urged his cock in to her with more force. "Feel how hard I am for you. What I'm going to fuck you with when we get back to our room." He tilted his head back so he could see her big brown eyes. Craving the moment when his next words hit her, made her clit throb and her abdomen ache. "The only thing I'm thinking about is your tiny black shorts and lacy panties down around your ankles, your pink pussy stretching around me as I take you deep."

Her gaze darkened with desire.

"You'd like that, wouldn't you, Dirty Girl?"

Her answer came in the form of her hands slipping down from around his neck to the curve of his shoulders, to the sensitive bones at the base of his spine. Her demand came when she snaked them around to his stomach. Her fingers tormented the muscles of his abdomen. She toyed with his belt buckle as she drove her pubic bone into his cock.

"If you don't stop teasing me, I'm going to fuck you right here."

She laughed, sticking a finger under his shirt and feathering it along the hair that led into his pants. "I'm pretty sure you want this to last longer than the two minutes it takes to get up to the fifth floor, don't you?" Her lashes fluttered against her cheeks.

He certainly did, but he also wasn't going to waste a minute of the one time he could fuck her, either. And if she was in the mood to tease, he was going to tease.

He upped the ante, slipping a hand down her shorts, beneath her panties, slicking his finger against her silky skin. Fuck, he wanted her now. But he also wanted to see her, all of her, lying naked and waiting for him, spread open on that beautiful white bed.

He found her clit and twirled his fingertip around it. "I'm going to make sure your pussy is all juicy and swollen for me." He stuck a finger inside her.

She squealed that same squeal of fear, delight, and need he recalled from the closet. That sound was the sound he was chasing. He thrust his finger into her again and she pressed her lips against his shoulder, muffling her cry.

"You like that, Dirty Girl?"

She moaned into his shoulder, her strangled breath the only answer he needed to hear.

"You are so tight." He continued to slide his finger in and out. "My cock is wailing to be inside you."

The doors opened with a *ding* as if luck were answering his prayers.

He stepped back so she could gather herself, while he tried to put himself together, too. He would keep this a secret. He would obey her every rule.

But God, did he want to carry her to their room with her legs wrapped around his waist, kissing her until both of them became so lost that only the touch of the other would help them to be found again.

"Oh no," Valerie groaned as they stepped out of the elevator.

He noticed the cause of her distress. The housekeeping cart was parked in front of their room, a vacuum blaring inside.

Fuck.

"We forgot the necktie." She attempted to smile. She took a deep breath even though he could sense her whole body shaking at the speed of a rabbit's heart.

No. Nothing was getting in the way of fucking her, this minute. *Soon* was not good enough. *Now* was the only choice.

"Ice and vending?" he asked, indicating the sign on the wall.

"Are you serious?"

He pressed his lips to her ear. "I know you've been fantasizing about me fucking you since last night. Do you really want to wait any longer?"

It came out bolder than he'd intended, but it was better

than his real thought. *I've been fantasizing about fucking you since last night, and I am not waiting one more second.*

She paused and looked from their room to him and back again. Maybe he'd gone too far.

"I can't wait any longer," she admitted, her eyes sheepish.

Had he ever heard sweeter words? He dragged her down the hall in the direction of the arrow on the vending sign, anticipation making him lightheaded.

They arrived at a fluorescent-lighted alcove. An ice machine and a Coke machine stood rumbling on either side of them.

It wasn't ideal. But there was a door they could close. They had enough room if they stood. "What do you think?"

She considered their surroundings. He should have just slammed the door and started up with her again. He was trying to be polite, and his question was going to make her bail.

"I'm more of a Pepsi girl"—she smiled slyly—"but what the hell?"

Surprise filled him, but was quickly extinguished by yearning as he closed the door and set his sights on her. "I'm going to make you a Coke girl."

She glanced at the closed door.

He pressed the back of his body against it. "No one is getting in here." He would keep that promise, but his position made it so she would have to come to him. "Get over here so I can ride that first rule out of you, Dirty Girl."

Instead of complying, she pushed the button on the ice machine and took a few cubes into her hands. "Remember when we would slip these down each other's shirts?"

She made her way over and he pulled her in. "It's not a memory anymore." He took a cube from her hand and shoved it down the front of her shirt.

She shrieked and jumped back. "You are not getting away

with that." She slipped the rest of the ice under his shirt, and he yelped.

He attempted to steady his breathing as she slid the ice along the muscles of his stomach. Ice-cold water dripped into his waistband, steaming his hot skin.

"You are asking for it." He popped a piece of ice in his mouth and slicked it against her neck and shoulders. Her body shuddered beneath the force of his cold tongue. He spit what was left across the room and used his teeth to pull the straps of her tank top and bra down.

"You might be able to do more with your lips than even I can," she breathed.

He ran his ice-cube-cold mouth over her already hard nipples. "You have no idea."

She arched, pressing her tits farther into his mouth as the rest of the ice cubes dropped to the floor at their feet. He continued to lick and suck at her, only taking a break to allow her to pull his shirt over his head. Before he could continue, though, she undid his belt, unzipped his fly.

Fuck, if he'd wanted her before, the fury with which she wanted him made his erection pulse. He moaned as her cold hands flitted over his abdomen and the *V* of his revealed boxers.

"You like that?" she asked, imitating his talk, and he was glad, because *fuck yeah I do*.

"Oh yeah, I like that a lot. How about you stroke my cock with one of those ice cubes?"

She paused.

"We get to tell each other what we want, remember?"

She nodded, went to the machine for a refill, and put her hand down his pants. The cold of the ice cubes against the blistering skin of his cock and her squeeze and tug at just the right pressure was taking him to the edge.

"Damn, have you done this before?"

"This, yes," she replied, hot in his ear. "Against a vending machine? No."

"Well." He reached for the button on her shorts. "I think it's time to tick something off your bucket list."

She pulled his pants down before he could get to her shorts. His cock bobbed, grateful to be free of his jeans. He was so hard it poked through the hole in his boxers.

She appraised his girth. Her eyes on him were almost as hot as her hands had been. They widened then glinted in focus.

She licked her lips. "I have something else I want to tick off first."

Oh fuck, he was pretty sure he knew where this was going. She kneeled in front of him, and he braced himself against the door.

She was lip level to his cock. It throbbed for the relief of her mouth slicking against it.

"Sucking me off was on your bucket list?" he managed.

"It's a recent addition."

She pulled his boxers down, slipped an ice cube into her mouth, and took him in, her lips hot and her mouth cold against his cock. She pulled back, sweeping her pink tongue along the tip, his rigid shaft still wet with her saliva.

"You know what they say about flute players, don't you?" she asked, taking the base of him into her hand.

He wanted to respond but he couldn't. His eyes were open but everything was black. Her breath against him, her lips that tight and firm and close were too much. He'd thought he was in charge of this, but fuck had he been wrong.

She owned him right now.

She took him into her mouth again, the cold making his legs shake and strain. She worked him slowly at first then took him deeper, so deep his head hit the back of her throat.

Whoever said that about flute players was right. Her

mouth was a master at any instrument it played. If he didn't take the power back, he was going to melt into a puddle on the floor with all that ice.

He anchored his hand on her ponytail to steady himself. Her expert lips slicked him faster, bobbing up and down the length of him. He was within minutes of coming, spraying hot against the back of her throat. While he wanted to, wanted her to suck him off and swallow everything he gave her, he wanted to come inside her more. He wanted to see that pussy. He wanted to fuck her now.

He drew her off of him. Her eyes glanced up, confused, her lips deliciously swollen.

"Dirty Girl, I want so badly to fuck your perfect flute-player mouth, but more than that I want to fuck your sweet, ripe pussy."

"I know, but—"

"Your mouth should be illegal," he interrupted. "I can only imagine what your pussy will be like."

She cocked her head, letting the words hit her.

"Show it to me," he urged. "Show me everything."

She rose and removed her shirt and bra from where they were hitched around her stomach. She didn't pause as she unbuttoned her shorts, following his every demand.

"Slower," he said, giving her another one.

She took her shorts down and kicked them off to the side, waiting in her white lace underwear for his next command. Fuck, she was gorgeous. His eyes followed every line, dipped into every curve, longed to see the still hidden parts of her. The pussy he'd waited to see in full view until he fucked her was about to be unveiled to him—only to him.

"Say something." Her voice brought him back from the trip her body was taking him on.

Could he tell her what he thought of her? No, because he felt those words in his chest. He needed to keep this to what he felt in his pants.

"I'm just picturing what your wet panties are going to look like balled up on the floor next to us when I sink my cock into you."

She seemed relieved, and he knew his instincts were right. She'd asked him to treat her like a woman he fucked. He needed to remember that.

He flicked his chin at her. "Let's find out."

She slipped them off and waited. She was perfectly manicured, a whisper of fine brown hair in a tiny *V* on her pubic bone. Her hips were curved and ivory white like angel wings opening to him. She moved to cover herself.

"No." He motioned for her to drop her hands. "I need to see you."

Her whole body seemed to blush.

"Fuck, Dirty Girl," he murmured, words the only thing securing him to that space. He was spinning, dizzy from just looking at her.

She stood in front of him with her arms at her sides, like she was unsure what to do next. Oh, he would tell her. He was searching his mind for the words, when something else dropped in.

"Crap," he said. "My condoms are in the room." *Fuck, fuck, fuck.* They were here, naked, beyond turned on, and he couldn't do shit about it.

"Not a problem," Valerie said with a smile. She bent down for her shorts and pulled a shiny wrapper from the pocket.

He clicked his tongue, a wave of warmth coming on so strong it almost knocked him over. "You really are a dirty girl, aren't you?"

Instead of answering, she passed the condom over.

He ripped it open, slipped it on, and reached for her. "You have no idea what is coming your way," he growled, pressing his naked body to hers. His tongue licked along the edges of her lips as he entered her, going just as far as her rules would take him.

Her breath caught, and he sank deeper, trying to keep his own breath in check. Being inside her was demolishing him. He rocked against her slowly at first, enjoying the pull as she took him deeper and deeper.

He squeezed her ass. "Wrap your legs around me," he said as he hitched her up. She obliged and held him between her thighs in a perfect parallel to his thrusts.

Her arms were draped over his neck, her legs were around his waist, and her pussy was holding him, too. Each thrust she accepted seemed to clutch him tighter, bringing his desire to a boiling point. He wanted to kiss her so badly, needed to know what her swollen lips tasted like. He wasn't sure if it was because it was forbidden, or after seeing her work on his cock, he knew her kiss would be legendary. Or was it something even scarier? Even though he couldn't tell her how beautiful she was, how sexy, how rare, he wanted her to feel it. He bit her shoulder, fighting the urge to take her away in a kiss she would never be able to say no to.

"Fuck, your pussy feels so good," he said, going even deeper into the depths of her. "It's just as tight and luscious as I knew it would be."

Her breathing escalated, and he plunged faster to meet it.

"Are you ready to come for me?"

Her hands braced against the door, and he had his answer.

"I know how hard you can come. I tasted it earlier. I want to feel it this time. I want to feel you, bursting all over my cock."

She moaned again, her pussy engulfing him in a hot furnace of desire.

He was controlling himself, but barely. "Tell me what it's going to take. Tell me how to make you come."

"Faster," she panted. "Harder. Don't stop, not even to

breathe."

That he could do. He thrust against her, his cock shoving as far as she would take him again and again and again and again. His legs strained in effort, his mind was heady with the heat of her, but he kept plunging until she clenched around him.

Her nails dug into his back, and he knew she was done for, but holy shit so was he. Her breath became moans, then his name, over and over like a chant he would hear in the deepest parts of him forever.

He slammed into her just as his release hit—cold like the ice cubes and hot like her lips and bottomless like their foreplay hadn't started just this weekend. That this need for her had been building since the second he saw her walk into the band room freshman year with her flute case and her little plaid skirt, her hair in a French braid.

He fell against her, and she ran her lips along his bare shoulder, catching her breath. He somehow tried to catch his. They were just the sounds their bodies made as she detached from him. He knew he needed to say something, but his mind was still reeling, still swirling with his release, with the echo of her cries. She was all that was inside him. The terrible memories he usually carried were drowned out by their now.

He was here with her and nowhere else.

He slipped the condom off and tossed it in the trash.

"I don't know about you," Val said, thankfully breaking the silence, "but I'm thirsty."

"Does that mean I turned you into a Coke girl?" he teased.

Still naked, she reached into the pockets of her shorts for change, and clinked it into the machine. Two sodas clunked out. She bent down to grab them, giving him a breathtaking view of her creamy ass. Even after being completely satisfied by her, all he could think about was burying his face in it. His cock threatened to go hard again. He reached for his boxers and pulled them on. He had done what she wanted, and they were finished.

Would he ever find the peace he felt when he was inside her again?

Maybe he would be able to convince her that this time hadn't counted because they weren't in a bed.

What the hell am I thinking?

She had ruined him, by saving him. But he couldn't let her know it. He would try to follow her rules even if it killed him.

She popped the top on both sodas and passed him one.

She took a sip and considered for a millisecond before spitting it out into the trash. "I may never see Coke the same way again." She laughed. "But that still tastes like crap."

Chapter Eight

When they reached the room, housekeeping was long gone. Valerie's thoughts that she could move on after that and act like nothing had happened were seemingly on their way out, too.

She rushed into the bathroom to clean up. She needed to breathe—wanted to be alone with her swirling thoughts. They seemingly whirred around in her brain like the bathroom fan above her.

Had that really happened? Had she actually had sex with Alec? Initiated a blowjob with him?

Her skin blushed on top of her afterglow, and she splashed cold water on her face. She did not act like that with men. She did not have sex in the vending machine rooms of hotels and she did not initiate blowjobs, but she'd loved every minute of it. She was still shaking with just how much.

She replayed his sexy words, his touch, his insanely expert thrusts, and hot-as-lava breath. Even so, it was good they hadn't been able to do it in their hotel room bed, because she would crave cuddling now. She would want to be against his chest, tracing the lines of his tattoos, while he murmured into her hair.

Alec was her best friend and seemingly willing to do whatever she wanted, but he was not that guy. He didn't cuddle, and he certainly didn't murmur into hair, not after he'd gotten what he wanted from the woman under that hair.

It was why she'd spoken first after they'd finished. Why she'd turned the attention to a stupid Coke, so he didn't suspect she'd even considered wanting him to be that guy.

She took a deep breath. She needed to stop. He'd never promised to be. He'd promised to screw her against a Coke machine until she orgasmed like an erupting geyser, and he'd more than kept his promise. So why couldn't she stop wondering what it might feel like to be in his arms now?

Control yourself, Valerie. You're the one who insisted this only be about sex. Remember?

She had rejected him ten years ago when he asked for more, and he would reject her now if she did. He had beautiful women lined up and waiting for him in L.A. Sure, he could stay faithful to her for one sexual tryst, but he could never stay faithful to her forever, commit to a life with her with a ring and a vow, not when he could have any gorgeous woman he wanted. He'd just seen every last bit of her and hadn't said a word about how she looked, which just increased her self-consciousness. Of course, he was her best friend—she couldn't expect him to lie.

When she finally stepped out of the bathroom, she found Alec lying on the just-made bed, strumming his guitar. His clothes were rumpled, his hair was a mess, but the look suited him.

These days few looks didn't. She'd been able to view him as impartially handsome for years, but now every time she saw him, it made her woozy. He was hot—too hot to be sitting in this room with her and too hot to be lying on their bed.

And most definitely too hot to have just done what he'd

done to her.

She sucked in a breath. He was still Alec. Even though his jaw, peppered with shiny brown stubble, and the way he bit his lip slightly as he strummed away made her crazy. He was still Alec. She said a prayer to the rock gods that he kept his shirt on.

"I haven't heard you play in so long," she finally said, not allowing herself to pause and think before joining him on the bed.

This was how things were supposed to be between them—casual, normal, no whirring thoughts filling her mind. No insatiable desire gnawing at her belly. She lay back and closed her eyes, floating away on the sound of his expert fingers on guitar strings.

His expert fingers… Her ears heated, realizing he hadn't cleaned up like she had, yet. She was still all over those fingers, and now she was a part of the music he was making. She wondered if he'd thought it, too, or if sex with her hadn't turned him into a total lunatic.

"Yeah." He didn't look up from the guitar. "FaceTiming our practice just isn't the same. Remember this?" He started playing the first notes of "Every Breath you Take" by The Police.

"I used to love when you'd play that." She closed her eyes, losing herself in the sound. It was the song he'd played for his senior solo in high school. Valerie could remember him practicing and practicing in the band room. Even when he was learning it, even when it was shaky, she'd lapped up every note. "It might be my favorite thing you've ever played."

He made an attempt to keep going, but when he missed a few chords and changes he stopped.

"I'm way rusty on that." He reset and noodled around a bit, finally playing a G into an A into an E and repeating them, weaving them into a song; the tempo was as slow as he had been when he was getting his footing with her against the vending machine room door.

Wow, maybe now she would only view her life as *B.F.* and *A.F.* Clearly she'd underestimated Alec's capabilities. He'd put some sort of spell on her. Maybe he *was* her sexual messiah, her personal Cock-fucius.

"What do you think of a B-minor for the chorus?" he asked, his fingers still strumming.

"Nice."

"It's new. I just started it last night."

The calm breaths she was attempting while in his proximity started to choke her. It could be coincidence, but she knew that like her—even more so than her—he used his music to feel.

What do those notes mean?

Why do I care?

"It's a lot sweeter than what you usually write," she said, pushing her thoughts aside. There was no doubt about that. If he was using music to illustrate his feelings, this song said *contentment*, plain and simple.

Chronic Disharmony was a rock band, and while their songs were catchy enough to hit the charts, they were way faster and harder than this.

Her abdomen clenched at the thought of those words—*faster, harder*. She couldn't believe she'd just said those words to him while he screwed her against a vending machine. Jeez, the song she would have written to show her feelings would probably be closer to "Flight of the Bumblebee."

No matter how much she tried, she was not as calm about this as he was. But then, he was used to this. Used to having his way and going away. That was how he'd always put it.

The memory of him inside her overtaking her, she saw the appeal.

"I have a reputation to protect." His expression was pure as he shifted the guitar. "Don't tell anyone." He chuckled.

"Sweet is not in Chronic Disharmony's wheelhouse."

Don't tell anyone, one of her rules. It brought a guilty acid into her stomach. She hadn't even been able to keep it. She'd demanded it of him and spilled the details to Cynthia the first chance she'd had. Now that she really knew what being fucked by Alec Rogers was like, would she ever be able to keep her mouth shut?

"I need to tell you something," she started.

"Uh-oh," he said, stopping mid-strum.

She sensed something in his gaze, fear or worry. It was not like Alec, and it only made her guilt surge.

"The condom wasn't mine."

He laughed, the sparkle returning to his eyes. "Considering what just happened, I was expecting something a lot worse. Like maybe you faked your orgasm, or I was the worst sex you'd ever had."

Is he kidding? If he could even think that was the worst sex she'd ever had, what kind of sex was he used to having? She decided to tackle his first statement and ignore his second. She was already having enough trouble forgetting about all the women in L.A. who came before her and all who would surely come after—she grimaced—*literally.*

"Um, no, my orgasm was definitely not fake." As she replied, the parties involved seemed to hum to life again, like just the word and him so close might mean it was imminent—*down, girl.*

"I didn't think so," he continued with light, easy laughter. "If so you missed your calling. You should have been in the drama club instead of band."

"Right." She managed to laugh, too, even as the guilt creeped up from her stomach to her throat. She needed to tell him. Tell him that she was the weak one.

"So, the condom was Cynthia's." She spoke quickly so he couldn't interrupt her before she got it all out. "And she gave it to me because I told her about you."

He lifted an eyebrow.

"About us," she added. "I'm sorry. I didn't mean to, it's just she was there last night when we were in the closet and—"

"Breaking one of your own rules?" he interrupted. "You certainly aren't leading by example."

He didn't seem angry, but that didn't change the way breaking what she now viewed as *their* promise made her feel. Telling Cynthia took her right back to high school again—sharing sticky gossip just so she didn't explode from knowing it. That was how it had felt that morning, and maybe part of why she'd told was that she couldn't go to Alec. She'd needed a confidante and it couldn't be him anymore, not about this.

"You're seriously not mad?"

"You're going to have to do better than that to get me angry, Val. When women kiss and tell with me, or *not* kiss and tell"—he winked—"it's not with one of their best friends from high school. It's usually with the *Enquirer*. I'm fine."

Val stared at him. He was way better at dealing with all of this than she was. Not that she was surprised.

"Besides, knowing Cynthia like I do, she's trustworthy," he continued. "So, sure, tell her all about it. Tell her everything I just did to you." His voice went low. "Every sordid detail."

He leaned closer to her, close enough to kiss, close enough that she could smell herself on him. She understood it was not unintentional. Perhaps he was seeing if she'd break yet another of her rules, or perhaps he was letting her know he could tell she sort of wanted to.

"You can tell someone, too," she said instead, pulling back slightly. If she kissed him right now, she was going to climb on top of him and force him to make that noise. That strangled breath he'd made when he entered her. Like her body and air was all he needed in this world. "I mean"—she pulled back from him even farther—"if you want to."

He smiled and reached for his phone, clicked into it, and stared at the screen. "She was expecting me to tell her you said hi, too, not this, but what the hell?"

"Not your mom!" she screamed, slapping the phone out of his hand.

"For someone so intelligent and driven, you are still insanely gullible." He smiled, his eyes running over her face, his pale lips puckering slightly.

She couldn't blink. She couldn't even breathe. She could do nothing but get lost in the way he looked at her. Had he always looked at her this way?

"Sorry, I'm not thinking as clearly as usual." Of course he wasn't going to tell his mom. *Seriously, Val, get it together.*

"Any reason why?" he pressed, even though his deep brown eyes told her he knew.

She wanted to hold his gaze, but she couldn't. She looked down at her hands, her now seemingly useless hands.

"Hey." He patted her leg. "We're just two best friends hanging out on a bed together. You can tell me anything."

"We aren't supposed to talk about it," she said, chastising herself as the words came out. But Alec did this to her. His warm and open face, his calm and sweet ways had tricked her into saying exactly what she shouldn't have said.

"Ah, you'll just think about it until it makes you crazy—good plan." He waited, leaving the door open.

She could share the way she felt right now, but what was she going to say? Better and worse than she ever had. More certain and more confused than she'd even known were possible.

Thankfully he started playing again after a minute of silence. He knew her well enough to fill their empty spaces, which seemed so much emptier now, with music.

Music was just one of the languages they used that no one else understood. Another was how with only a look, they could know exactly what the other was thinking. She wondered if

Alec could tell. If, even though she was choosing not to speak, he could see every shooting synapse of her mind. Every part of her that wondered, *what if?*

He stopped strumming with a start and turned to her. "Why didn't you ever come and visit me?"

Crap. Even though it wasn't what she'd been thinking, she knew it was something he'd always wondered. He'd asked her to stay with him in his big L.A. mansion. Invited her to shows over and over the first few years he was in the band. After a while he stopped because who wants to be rejected all the time? Especially when she'd dished out that first rejection that had almost ruined their friendship.

"I always thought you were too busy," she replied. She could never say the real reason. If he saw her next to the women who hung on him, was able to compare face to face, breasts to breasts, ass to ass, he might not bother with her anymore. Even as a friend. She thought of the ex-cheerleaders who were hanging all over him that morning. It was how she'd felt next to them in high school. How she'd felt alone at night in her room when she heard the echoes of their taunts.

Barking.

The nickname stuck even as she got her braces off, grew into her gangly body, and her skin cleared. No matter what she did, it followed her like a suffocating shadow. She hated how she'd been cut down by a stupid nickname. She hated how, being back with all these people, she still could be.

"That's a terrible excuse, Val."

"You could have come to visit me," she tried. Better he see her stacked up against other women in the symphony. Women she could actually compete with.

His eyes went dark, his usually proud chin lowered. "I know," he said. He had his own reasons for staying in L.A. Reasons she knew were probably the same as some of her own. They didn't belong together in the real world, even as friends. He was famous and beautiful and she was plain and normal, numbingly normal, and putting them in the same room would only illustrate that.

The only reason it hadn't yet this weekend was because this was not the real world.

But there were also the secrets she knew about him. The secrets that might have been the real reason he'd never come to visit her. She knew his past better than anyone, she knew that he'd tried to give himself to her, and she knew that she'd said no.

"We could start visiting each other now," he suggested.

"What's changed?" she asked before she could stop herself. She didn't need him to reply; the answer was *everything*.

"Well, I'll be in L.A. for six months recording our next album, and now that I've been in the same room with you again," he said, his gaze intensifying so fiercely his dimple shook, "FaceTime is not going to cut it."

She swallowed.

"I should have insisted on seeing you before now."

She managed a laugh. "You've never been able to make me do anything."

He looked away, his hand circling the neck of his guitar. Was he thinking about that day? The day he'd left for New York, the day she'd said no?

She'd apologized so many times when she was trying to get him to speak to her again, but it was clear it still hurt him. When someone as closed off as Alec finally opens the door and gets it slammed shut, does he ever really recover?

"We can go to the beach," he said, thankfully bringing the subject back to her visit. "You'll love it."

"Sounds perfect," she said, leaning back on the pillow, trying to picture walking along the beach with him. Would they hold hands?

"And don't worry, when you come to L.A. your rule about

being the only woman in my life will still apply."

Was he saying what she thought he was saying? Did she want him to be saying it?

"It'll be just you and me hanging out for as long as you want to stay," he continued.

Hanging out. No, he wasn't saying what she thought he was saying. He was being polite. It made her a little sick that she'd even thought he could see her that way now.

"I'm there, unless I'm in London." Her response was two-pronged. To remind her to forget those fantasies and to indicate to him that she had better things to do than just *hang out.*

"London." Alec's eyes went dark. "I guess I forgot."

Was he upset she might be going? Would he have been two days ago?

"They have cell phones in London."

His gaze met hers, the doubt in his eyes hypnotizing seconds into minutes. "I guess FaceTime is going to have to cut it," he finally said.

Her mouth turned to dust. Was he working to forget some fantasies, too?

She glanced at the clock, anywhere to escape his eyes. "We're going to be late for cocktails." She couldn't believe how the afternoon had gotten away from her, from them.

Alec stood, walked over to his suitcase, and pulled out a three-quarters-full bottle of vodka. It must have been what he was using to fill his flask.

"No, we're not." He smiled. "Also, I think I know where we can get some ice and mixers."

She managed to smile back, but her face was on fire, and the hairs at the back of her neck poked out like needles. That room, the feeling of him rocking inside her when they were in that room, was all she could see.

"Not Coke," she replied quickly.

He laughed.

"I'm seriously never going to like Coke."

"I did my best." He fluttered his eyelashes.

That brought a laugh from her. "Pretty sad even *that* couldn't flip me."

He paused, straightened his shoulders, and finally cleared his throat. "Does this mean we're talking about it? Because I don't know about you, but I'd really like to."

She tried to breathe. *He wants to talk about it?* Maybe she'd had him all wrong. Maybe he was the guy who wanted to cuddle and murmur into her hair. *Crap, why can't I stop thinking about that?*

"I guess," she said, needing to say something.

"I'm not going to get crazy on you or anything, but I always talk to you about the women I'm with. What happened between us shouldn't change that."

She understood what he was doing, but in that moment she didn't care. She wanted to relive it with him. God knew she'd be reliving it with herself nightly, and whenever she had the time to take a bath.

"Okay." She reached out for the bottle, needing a little liquid courage.

He headed to the bed and handed it over, taking a spot beside her. He sat back against the headboard and laid his black-jeaned legs out in front of him.

She took a swig, the familiar burn calming her.

"For starters"—his eyes were tight on hers—"you give a fucking amazing blowjob."

She almost spit the vodka all over him. She swallowed her drink and stared. She knew when someone gave you a compliment you were supposed to say "thank you" but she couldn't. It was too much.

He didn't speak; he was forcing her to.

Grasping for anything, she finally said, "Who are you

comparing me to?"

His face pinched.

She was trying to give him the crap she always did, but clearly she'd miscalculated. "Sorry, I was joking." She shrugged. "I guess I don't know how to do this."

He exhaled. "You talk to me about guys all the time." His fingers widened on the bedspread.

All the time was not that accurate. He talked to her about women, and she said whoever she was seeing at the moment was "fine." She never gave details. He asked for them and sometimes she acquiesced, but for the most part he told her things.

Things she saw now had been fueling what had just happened between them more than she'd realized.

"Here's a tip." He took a finger and tapped it against the center of her nose. "When I'm telling you how sexy you are, don't bring up other women."

"Right," she replied, feeling a blush down to her bones.

"You could reply with your own compliment about how sexy I am," he suggested with a lighthearted smile, "or…" His face turned serious, his eyes had the power to give her a heart attack. "You could just say thank you."

She took another drink, the warmth of the vodka not even coming close to the heat on her skin as she rewound back to the two of them in that room. She passed the bottle back, she'd had enough. She could barely control herself sober.

"I do think you're sexy," he admitted, his shoulders wide against the headboard. "I know I need to try and forget that, but it's the truth."

She swallowed and stared at him. He'd told her to say thank you. He'd told her to reply with her own compliment, but even now she was still too insecure to say anything at all.

He moistened his lips. "One day I'm going to make you take that compliment."

She exhaled, letting out the words she could let out. "I

wanted to keep going with that blowjob," she said, forcing herself to see his reaction. His eyes seemed to gloss over, like he was right back to her mouth tight around him. "I wanted to play you like you played me this morning."

"Really?" He ran his fingers through his stubble. "Tell me more."

She wasn't sure she could. Not when they were sitting like this, like friends, on a bed together. When he called her *Dirty Girl* and had his hands all over her, she could say the words he demanded from her. But now...

"You first," she said.

He didn't hesitate. "When I was inside you"—the bed squeaked slightly as he leaned closer to her, so close his sturdy frame could have swallowed her up—"I forgot where I was for a minute." There was vodka on his breath, lust in his eyes. "It, you, felt so fucking good. It was like I was nowhere and everywhere."

How am I going to top that? She couldn't. Instead she just said, "Me too."

He ran the lip of the bottle along his own lips, took a long drink. "It's too bad that was a onetime thing." The words came out as a tease. "I'd really like to let you finish that blowjob."

She wanted to laugh from nervousness, but she forced herself to sit still. His eyes traveled along her face, down to her lips, and she couldn't help but lick them in response.

Could she just bend over and take him into her mouth? Valerie didn't do things like that on her own. Alec's touch brought out that side of her. Clearly she needed him to, because she was motionless.

She hoped he might make her be his Dirty Girl again, now. In fact she was screaming inside for how much she wanted him to. For him to say, *Show me how it feels to come in your mouth, Dirty Girl.*

But he didn't move. He just sat there, teasing his lips along the mouth of the bottle, making her crave his kiss even more. Making it clear she would have to make the first move.

She understood that if the rule was going to be broken, he was going to force her to be the one to break it.

Wow, did she ever want to. Her body simmered at the thought of having him in her mouth, controlling his pleasure, teasing and sucking at him until he came at the back of her throat. Letting him know what an amazing fucking blowjob she could really give, but if she was confused now, what would another round of the hottest sex she'd ever had in her life with her best friend be like?

She had to go back to being just his friend after this weekend, if she finally went to visit him in L.A. and had to stand next to all those other women. If she craved him again like this now, more of Alec would only make her crave him more.

"Yeah," she managed to choke out, "too bad."

He took another drink and stared at her for a long minute, the deep brown of his eyes lightening slightly as they started to water. He gave her one last chance before he got up and headed toward the bathroom. "I'm going to shower, if that's cool."

He closed the door behind him, and the moment was gone.

She'd let it slip by, but it was for the best. She heard the water turn on, and she continued to try and convince herself of that.

As a reminder of her real life, she picked up her phone and checked her email. What she was waiting for there was what she wanted—the only thing before this weekend that she'd ever wanted this badly.

The London Philharmonic. But her inbox still didn't hold an email from them. After this weekend, if she finally got London, would she still want Alec? Would he ever be able to commit to more than just wanting her? Would she ever be able to admit she needed him to?

Chapter Nine

Reece Freedland swung two golf putters in her hand. "You guys didn't finish the obstacle course. You missed the catered barbecue lunch," she droned on, "and you missed cocktails." A miniature windmill whirled behind her. A "waterfall" dripped into a "lake" the size of a baby pool at her side.

Valerie's classmates were picking up putters and dividing into teams divided by colored ball, but she and Alec were getting reprimanded while Cynthia stood beside them trying to keep her laughter in check.

"Were you taking attendance?" Alec shot back with a sly smile.

Valerie fought her own laugh attack, knowing it would only anger Reece further. She also had to admit she enjoyed Alec being her hero when it came to combating her ex-bully Reece Freedland, anyway.

Reece handed over the putters. "You two are playing miniature golf." An open-air arcade screamed with sound from behind her, phantom guns and lasers mingling with her voice. "And you are playing in round one so I know you participate."

The metal of the putter was hot and damp in Valerie's hand. Val liked to win, she was competitive in everything she did, but miniature golf was a toy not a game.

"We paid ahead of time for all of this, though, right? So if we choose to waste our money, that's our choice, our loss," Val tried.

Reece looked like her head was going to pop off.

Everyone had changed so much since high school, but Reece was the same—controlling, type-A Reece. Of course, Valerie had allowed Alec to leave the bed and take a shower instead of finishing what he'd called her *fucking amazing blowjob*. Even when he was dropping hints so hard she could get a concussion, she was still dorky, knock-kneed, stringy-haired Val.

It wasn't only confidence stopping her. It was her rules. She needed them. If she didn't have the assurance to be the woman Alec thought she was, she wasn't strong enough to be with someone like Alec.

"You are playing. On different teams," Reece added with a knowing smile.

That was what Val got for talking back. She'd wanted to be on Alec's team to prove they could do normal things and act normally together. She needed to know that her rules would stick.

Cynthia raised her hand. Her long blue peasant skirt and matching boho tank top made her appear like a Victorian beggar in Reece's presence. "Can I be on Val's team?"

Why was she bothering to ask? Seriously, Cynthia could do whatever she wanted. They all could. Reece was not the boss of them. But even as they protested, they stood there, listening, taking her crap.

"Of course." Reece smiled. "Alec," she added, eyeing him, "you can be on a team with—"

"Can't play." Alec stood taller in his boots. "My hands are insured for five hundred thousand dollars. I can't fuck them up."

He wore distressed jeans with holes in the knees and a tight white T-shirt. A different one than he'd worn the first night, but man, it was still perfection. Could people have their T-shirts and jeans tailored? Or did everything just fit Alec like it was an extension of his body?

"You're going to hurt your hands playing miniature golf?" Reece asked.

"Honey, you have no idea what I can do with a stick."

Cynthia tittered.

Valerie's ribs played her stomach like a bagpipe. She did know, intimately. Oh man did she know. She also knew what he could do with those hands, and she wasn't at all surprised they were insured for half a million dollars. Honestly, that was a bargain.

None of them spoke for a long minute. Reece was not backing down.

"I can call my manager if you'd like." Alec leaned the putter against his leg and pulled out his cell. "The reunion would be liable, of course," he continued, "if anything happened. I doubt you'd want to deal with that."

Reece squinted. "You won't have excuses for everything," she declared as she walked away.

"Bravo!" Cynthia clapped.

"Thanks for saving us, too," Val said sarcastically.

"What kind of saving did you have in mind?" Alec asked, his eyes daring her to look away.

Her ribs had moved on from her stomach and were beating against her heart in what felt like a caffeine-induced drum solo. What part of her body was going to betray her next? She clearly needed a break from Alec. Some time to breathe, to think. Like she hadn't been thinking enough already—well, *fantasizing.*

When she didn't respond, Alec thankfully, mercifully, continued. "Guess I'll see you ladies at the bar after." He started to head in when he paused and stepped closer to Valerie, moved his lips to her ear. He handed her his putter. "Take good care of my stick."

She thought he might say something else. *Dirty Girl,* or, *Like I know you can,* but Cynthia was standing there, watching them, her eyes as wide as the golf balls that littered the AstroTurf below them. Instead he just ran a finger down the length of her arm, tapping twice on the bone of her wrist, before heading into the bar.

Heat pooled between her legs. *Good God, how am I supposed to stop fantasizing now?* How was she supposed to not lead him by his fat silver belt buckle behind that tiny windmill?

As he walked away, Valerie thought of the picture of him in *Rolling Stone* highlighting his back and ass. It had nothing on seeing it in person—sculpted and taut and as flawlessly smooth as an apple. Forget about tailored jeans. Alec had a tailored ass.

"Seriously, can you guys bottle that? I need a heavy dose," Cynthia swooned.

Valerie managed a laugh. "You don't want it, believe me." But she was dizzy from him and awake in her panties. She should have worn a longer skirt like Cynthia's. Her knee-length black skirt and heels left her too exposed, allowed the part of her that had begged for Alec to be that much closer to open air.

Cynthia lifted an eyebrow. "You sure about that?" Her eyes glanced over Val's shoulder. "And what the hell is going on *there*?"

Valerie turned and found Gideon with his arms around Georgia, guiding her in a putt. Reece might have assigned their team, but it definitely seemed suspect they were together again. Those two wouldn't have been in the same galaxy in high school. Gideon had been president of the computer club and Georgia had been and was, well, Georgia. But now he was touching her, in public.

Maybe everyone had changed since high school. She heard Reece yelling about having to stay on schedule and noticed Randy Tines heading toward the bar. Well, everyone but herself and Reece.

"Don't ask me," Valerie finally replied.

"I swear it's like Cupid is on meth."

Valerie laughed. "Those two definitely don't seem to be among his best work."

"Seriously, though." Cynthia shook her head. "People are hooking up like frogs are raining from the sky."

Valerie noted there were an awful lot of men and women paired off on teams together, teams that Reece would have never concocted in her entire life.

"What about you?" Valerie cajoled. She needed someone else's gossip. She was drowning in her own.

"Not yet." Cynthia's eyes turned devilish. "But I have hope." She picked up a red golf ball. "All this practice with balls and ropes has to be good for something, right?"

Valerie couldn't control her burst of laughter. "If you want to hook up with someone, I'm sure you can. Like you said, Cupid is here. He might be on meth"—she snorted—"but he's definitely working."

Valerie glanced at the bar. It had huge garage-door-size windows, pushed up to let in summer air like the arcade. Alec sat inside with a beer. His silhouette was pensive as he ran his finger along the lip of his glass.

That finger... She throbbed where it had touched her, leaked from where it had entered her. She wasn't sure about Cupid, but the patron saint of *Playgirl* magazine was definitely in attendance.

Cynthia rolled her eyes. "Slobbering with the same guys I could have hooked up with in high school. Who wants that?" She pointed at Gideon and Georgia. "I want whatever funky weirdness is going on over there."

"Seriously, Cynthia, if there's someone you want…" She paused, not believing how casual she sounded. Everything seemed casual until *A.F.*, when every word became innuendo and every touch became fire. "All you'd have to do is ask."

"I don't want to ask. I want to be wooed. I want some guy I could have never been with in high school to tell me to take care of *his* stick!" She was yelling now. Not loud enough for other people to notice, but it was clear she meant it.

"Alec and I probably could have hooked up in high school," Valerie said, only to make Cynthia feel better.

But when Cynthia looked up at her, eyes blazing, she'd realized her lie hadn't worked. "Alec is a different deal altogether. He's a rock star now. He's not the geeky guy who used to follow you around like a puppy dog anymore."

"He never followed me around like a puppy dog." She couldn't say, *he's just like he was back then,* because who was she kidding?

"You can rewrite history all you want." Cynthia lifted her hand. "But I'm telling you no matter what is happening between the two of you now, that boy wanted you then."

Valerie had pushed it off at the time. Hadn't been ready for it, but Alec's invitation to New York City had been more than friendly. He'd offered her his heart that day the only way he knew how. But what they were doing now didn't have anything to do with that. They might have slept together. They might still have been able to joke around like they always did, but he wasn't offering her anything beyond a good time and certainly not the ultimate commitment she craved. Her rules made sure he never would.

Was she more afraid that sliver of feeling from the day after graduation would open again, or slam shut forever?

"Cupid was on target with you two," Cynthia countered.

"Cupid has nothing to do with it," Val responded. "It was just sex," she made herself add, needing the reminder. "And we're not doing it again."

"Wow." Cynthia took in Val's admission. "Why the hell not?" Her eyes were slits.

"It's complicated."

"You guys want each other, so what the hell is complicated about that?"

"That!" Val exclaimed. "That's what's complicated. And it's a rule, we made rules. We're only doing it once."

"It? Sex, you mean?" Cynthia corrected. "You could do other things, though, right?"

Val's eyes narrowed.

"I mean if we learned anything from Bill Clinton, sex is dick inside vagina, and there are many ways to get around that word."

Was Cynthia Cupid now? Because otherwise how could she know the unfinished business on Valerie's mind? Maybe she was right. A blowjob wasn't sex. Alec had taken care of her similarly that morning, and he'd said himself it hadn't counted. Maybe she needed to finish that unfinished business to finally get over Alec. She shook her head—if she believed that, someone could probably sell her a bridge in Brooklyn. But what other solution did she have?

"We should probably start playing or Reece is going to come back," Valerie said, pushing all those thoughts away.

"Nice save." Cynthia stepped up to the hole and set down the ball. She whacked it with far more force than she needed to up the green. It chucked against the wall and boomeranged toward her, landing right back in the tee area. "This game is going to take forever."

Val took her turn, and it was similarly dismal. Maybe this was why she hated miniature golf—she stunk.

"You know," Cynthia said as she took another shot. It banked against the opposite wall, but it landed in the middle of the green. "Not talking about something doesn't make it go away, Val."

Was Cynthia crawling around in her brain? Alec had tried to talk to her earlier about never coming to visit, about wanting her to visit now. She could have asked him what he really meant by her being the only one in L.A. She could have demanded that she be. Instead they'd both chickened out and talked about blowjobs.

Valerie didn't reply, just took her own shot. It hit the back wall of the hole and ricocheted past her to the bucket of balls behind them, knocking it over. "That should count for a hundred points."

"Don't change the subject." Cynthia clenched her jaw. "There's little I'm thankful for concerning my divorce, but one thing I did learn, when you keep things in, they explode."

"I'm not keeping anything in." The lie was like acid on Valerie's tongue, but she was keeping it in for her own good. Cynthia had not only been divorced, but married, too. She'd had a man declare he wanted her, only her, for the rest of his life—even if it hadn't lasted. That was the kind of relationship Valerie should have been working on and why she needed to let this thing with Alec go.

"Let me put it another way. If you deny yourself what you want, you will regret it." She didn't make it any secret as she glanced across the holes at Jacob Riedel. "God knows, I do."

"Cynthia." Valerie touched her hand. "You didn't get Jacob during spin the bottle?"

Cynthia shook her head. "I got Randy Tines, twice." She shuddered.

Valerie wrinkled her nose. "I would say I'm sorry, but

nothing is going to make that better."

"It was horrible," she said. "He kisses like you're his science experiment and he failed chemistry."

"Wow." She flashed to Alec's lips, full and mischievous. They had literally brought her to her knees. She hadn't even kissed him yet. *What is wrong with me?* She was never going to. If she kissed him she was going to want more. She wanted more already.

"I'm guessing Alec's lips don't feel like two wet rubber bands, so you might as well enjoy whatever is going on between you two right now."

"I told you it's complicated."

"Were you happier before you got to the reunion, or now?" Cynthia asked.

"Now," Val admitted. She didn't even have to think. For the first time all weekend, the answer was right there sitting across her line of sight at the bar.

Chapter Ten

Alec nursed his beer. The stools up at the bar were decorated to look like pool balls and a table was in use behind him. The soft *thwack* of the balls as they hit felt and slid into velvet pockets was a welcome theme song; anything was better than the buzzing in his head.

Honestly, he would have played stupid miniature golf, even with Reece's obnoxious demands, but he needed to gather himself when it came to Val.

Right now, he was anything but gathered.

He was uncontrollably replaying every sensual moment they'd had and trying to figure out how he could convince her to repeat any and all of them. But she'd stipulated only one time, and he'd given it to her. Even if he couldn't think about anything else, it was done. It wasn't just sex, either; he wanted the after, too. He craved what they'd denied themselves, holding her, kissing the top of her head as she lay against his chest.

But she didn't want that. Her rules—their past made that abundantly clear.

He took a sip of his beer, hoping the calmness would come. Welcoming the numbness he craved, the numbness he'd gotten used to. Maybe he couldn't get her out of his mind because he wasn't blackout drunk. That, at least, he could control.

Or he could have, if Valerie wasn't on the hole directly across from him. She was bent over in concentration, her heels digging into the AstroTurf, her skirt riding up her thighs as she eyed a shot. His cock shifted as she bent lower, her tight ass calling out like a fucking beacon. The way she touched him, lay her lips on his shoulder, was everything he ever wanted in the world.

His eyes remained on her, and condensation fogged his beer glass. He needed to get a fucking clue. She didn't want him, and he didn't deserve her. Not ten years ago, and not now.

He forced himself to look away before she had him in orbit, pulled him across the bar and all the holes and into her arms.

What the hell is happening to me? All he knew was that now that he'd had a taste of Val, he couldn't stop.

Could he not get her out of his mind because he'd known her forever, or was it because in the portion of his heart he usually crammed down, he wondered if maybe he could know her forever?

Know her as his Val and his Dirty Girl, the best of both worlds, the *best*.

But how could he even be considering that? When he'd offered her even a small taste of forever ten years ago, she'd rejected him. He was not the guy who could give her the promise she dreamed of, and she knew it.

He'd panicked at the thought of going to New York alone. His whole life he'd wanted to escape, but when he had it in his hands, the uncertainty was too much. The only certain thing in his life up to that point had been Valerie. He'd begged her to come to keep that certainty, that security. He'd asked for himself and not for her.

When she'd said no, it cemented what he always knew. What he still believed. Forever was for other people. For people who hadn't grown up with his parents' marriage — his father staying because he had nowhere else to go and his mother staying because she was too scared to leave — he bearing the guilt and weight of it all.

He pushed the thoughts away and attempted to enjoy the beer in his hand, the quiet he hoped it would bring to his mind, when Randy Tines strode up next to him.

Guess Reece had lost another of her flock.

"Alec!" He slapped his back sloppily and stumbled as he took the stool next to him.

Randy was clearly using this weekend for debauchery. Not that Alec should talk. Randy's antics didn't come close to what Alec got up to most nights, and his behavior was encouraged by the other guys in Chronic Disharmony, his manager, and the women who let him keep his life squarely in the now.

"Midget golf." Randy groaned. "Who the hell put Reece in charge of this thing?"

"She did."

Randy let out a long booming guffaw.

Alec missed being around people who really knew him. Not like he and Randy were close in high school, but the history they shared linked them. The guys in the band were great, but they only knew a certain kind of Alec. He gave them the past he'd always wanted rather than miring them in his truth. They didn't know about his mom, they definitely didn't know about his dad, and he never talked to them about anything besides the unholy trinity of bands — sex, drugs, and rock and roll.

Only Valerie knew his real story, the shitty ashes he'd risen from and the way he carried them in his chest like an urn. Maybe that was why her touch haunted him like a ghost in racy lingerie.

"Besides," Alec added, "no one else wanted to be in charge."

"Good point." Randy spit his *P*. He leaned in conspiratorially. "If I was running this thing we'd be doing a whole lot more of what we did last night."

Alec's mind reeled at the mention. He knew it had only been the night before when they'd played Seven Minutes in Heaven, but it seemed like weeks had passed. Between him and Valerie everything changed, or *had changed*. Why did he keep forgetting it was only going to happen once?

Because he wanted to forget. Because he hoped she might break another of her rules.

"You definitely found your calling."

"I know." Randy grew more animated. "I call myself the closet Casanova. Worked with you two, didn't it?"

Alec shook his head and was about to correct him, but Randy continued. He was the kind of drunk where talking was the only thing rooting him in reality. "Fate had put you guys together years ago, but you"—Randy pressed his finger into Alec's shoulder—"were too much of a pussy back then. Fate knew it would have another chance. Last night, Fate took it."

"You have no fucking clue what you're talking about."

Pussy he was not. He'd tried to make something with Valerie. Sure, he hadn't known what he was asking for, but he'd tried. Fate had been the one who fucked that up.

But it was hard to deny that it seemed like Fate was giving them a second chance. Valerie had just broken up with someone. He wasn't really involved with anyone at the moment. He'd told her for some reason, just before they walked into a game of Seven Minutes in Heaven, that she needed to get her brains fucked out to forget her ex-boyfriend, and when she "spun the bottle" it had landed on him. Fuck. If it wasn't Fate, or whatever, it was one fucking insane coincidence after another.

If what had happened between them was fated, shouldn't it keep happening?

Or was Val's request for only one encounter Fate, too? Life letting him know he would continue to get kicked in the balls when it came to love. Not that he'd ever tried to make friends with love in the first place.

Love? Fuck, he wasn't drunk enough to be throwing words like that around, even in his head.

"You can thank me at your wedding." Randy wobbled on his barstool.

"That is never happening," Alec said quickly. His face heated, and clammy sweat clung to his skin.

A wedding was Valerie's dream, not his—and not with *him*. That was why no matter what feelings she was starting to ignite in him, he needed to keep dousing them out. The point of every casual relationship he'd ever had was to run away from that word—the prison that his mother still lived in.

Only Val knew that. Val, the person who Randy thought he should marry. He took a long drink.

"Another round," Randy said to the bartender, indicating their empty glasses. "On his tab."

Alec tilted his head. This guy had serious balls.

"What? I know you can afford it, and since I won't be at your wedding, you can give me that thank-you now."

"Whatever," Alec replied, giving a curt nod to the bartender. He could buy everyone at the reunion a beer if Randy was going to get technical about it.

"Dude." Randy tried to focus his bloodshot eyes on him. "It's too bad you're with Val now, because I am getting so much pussy at this reunion. It's like a vending machine."

Vending machine? Alec's cock pulsed, as if that term had turned it Pavlovian now.

But why the hell had Randy picked that word? Was he going to say he called the women he slept with *Dirty Girl* next? Of course, Alec had never called anyone that before Valerie. He knew he would never call anyone that again.

He remembered those old Hollywood movies where an angel was sent down to help the main character put his life into focus. He glanced at Randy Tines, sweaty, red-faced, a thick neck topped by a blond buzz cut you could use to scrub pots and pans. Randy was no angel. He proved that as he continued.

"Yeah, stick a compliment in about how much hotter they are since high school and bam, a pussy slides out."

"Congrats, man," Alec replied with zero enthusiasm.

"That must be what your life is always like, huh?" Randy considered. "Pussy as far as the eye can see—acres and acres. Instead of a vending machine, you have a twenty-four-hour pussy farm."

"Pretty close," Alec admitted quietly. Once the band took off, it had been a smorgasbord of willing, docile, seemingly sex-starved women who were eager to do whatever he wanted.

That had been his life; his uncomplicated, perfect life. But he was starting to see that those women were using him as much as he'd been using them. He was starting to see that he'd been treating those women like Band-Aids for a wound they could never heal. A wound that had started with his father's blows but had been opened by Valerie's rejection the day after graduation.

"It must be fucking great." Randy smiled wistfully.

That was when he noticed the gold wedding band glinting on Randy's finger. "You're married?"

"Not this weekend." Randy smiled, his teeth sticky with

beer.

"Fuck, man." Alec's voice went low, his jaw clenched. "You can't be doing that shit." His father had cheated on his mother for years. An abuser and a cheater and a liar, and yet his mother still stayed with him.

"Seriously? The guy with a pussy parade is telling me that."

"I'm not married," Alec said.

"That's because for the past fourteen years you and your *wife*," Randy hissed, "couldn't get up the balls to fuck each other until someone forced you."

Alec screeched his chair back, his muscles quivered and tensed. He wanted to knock the shit out of Randy Tines. He wanted to turn him into a sniveling stain on his barstool. But he didn't fight people. He'd been hit too many times to ever hit anyone, even someone who deserved it.

He turned to Randy and steadied himself. "Finish your fucking beer and get the fuck away from me."

Alec noticed a commotion coming from the front window of the bar; a few local news guys were setting up with cameras. He hated this part of fame.

Alec leaned over to the bartender. "Is there a place I can have a drink with no windows?" He glared at Randy. "Preferably alone?"

• • •

They set Alec up in the pinball room. People who weren't a part of the reunion were using it, and Alec had softened the blow by saying yes to their autographs and selfies and buying them all a round of drinks.

He'd let any fan who asked take a picture with him, have anything they wanted from him because they actually gave something back—energy or drive or inspiration.

The media was a different story; they just took. It reminded him of the way his father treated his mother. Taking, taking, taking, and giving nothing back but a roof over her head, from what Alec could see. That was why Alec had bought her the house, so maybe she'd stop letting his father take before there was nothing left.

Of course, his father also gave her things Alec couldn't see. Things he could hear, the same things he'd given Alec when he was too small to fight back. Things they'd both had to hide in long sleeves and pants even on the hottest summer days. When Alec got too big to hit anymore, his father seemed to go double time on his mother. While he wanted to stop him then, he also hoped his mother would do it—finally stand up to him, be strong enough to walk away for both of them.

She never did. So instead of blasting music as loud as he could in his bedroom to drown out the sound of her cries, he'd escape to Valerie's.

The guilt still ate at him. Yet another reason he'd bought the house for his mom. The house he would probably have to sell. It had been vacant for so long they were starting to have problems with vandalism. The neighbors were complaining, and it was in the kind of neighborhood where if someone didn't occupy it soon, he would have to let it go.

Lose his mother's one chance at escape because she wouldn't accept she needed it.

He had to try one last time. He stood up straighter and clicked his mother's number on his phone.

"How's Valerie?" she asked before he could even say hello.

He hadn't called to talk about Valerie; fucking Fate needed to mind its own fucking business.

"She's fine, she says hi," he managed.

"Oh, tell her I say hi, too." His mom's voice trilled with the excited pitch it got when she talked about Val.

His mom had always wanted them together. The minute she met Valerie when he was fourteen, she'd whispered, *Hold on to that one.*

At the time he'd responded, "Gross, Mom," with the signature whine that he carried until his deep baritone came in.

Could Fate have been working then, too?

"I already told her, Mom," he breathed, trying to keep his focus. "You texted when I got here, remember?"

"Oh, I know, but tell her I say hi again."

"Okay." He couldn't help but let out a chuckle at his mom's obvious quasi-daughter-crush. The laughter grew when he remembered Val's face as he gave her his mom's greeting in the elevator last night. Hopefully he'd have better timing sharing this latest one.

It was one of the only things his mom ever asked him to do once he left home, *say hi to Valerie* and *please come and talk to your father.*

The Valerie request had been the only thing he ever complied with. His parents lived in Maine now, moved onto his grandfather's old farm. He'd never been there. He would never go there.

He took a long breath, kneaded his fingers into his temple, anticipating the pounding pain he knew would come. Valerie would have had this conversation over with already. Might even have had his mom moved in and settled by now.

Communication: one of the other things his family wasn't big on.

"I'm going to see the house tomorrow. I wanted to make sure your garden is being taken care of." His fingers moved up to his forehead, the disgustingly familiar throb building in intensity. It hadn't been what he wanted to say. What he wanted to say was, *It is time for you to finally move into the home I bought you. It is time for you to finally leave him. It is time for you to be able to do what I was able to do.*

I am doing for you what you could never do for me.

His mother's garden was her one sanctuary. Dad could yell and push and squeeze her arms until there were worm-like welts on them behind the shielded walls of the house, but in the garden she was free. They both had been. As free as he'd felt in the band room or in Val's bedroom.

As free as he'd felt inside Val that day.

"Alec." She sighed. "It's not my garden, it's yours."

They'd had this fight, this passive aggressive fight, what seemed like hundreds of times now. Something about this time was supposed to be different if Fate were truly on his side.

Wouldn't his mom finally see? Wouldn't she finally say, *yes I'm ready. Get me away from this monster.*

Unfortunately, she also loved that monster in her own sick way. That monster was her husband, his father. He paced the floor trying to think of a response, but there wasn't one. There was only what he wanted and what she was not willing to do.

Instead of doing what he'd asked, what he'd begged her to do, she chose to stay with the man who'd made his life hell for eighteen years.

"I'm going to have to sell it if you don't move in," he said. It was a new addition to their conversation, but she had to suspect it was coming.

Besides, he needed her to know this wasn't going to be her somewhere over the rainbow forever. If she didn't take it now, it would be gone.

"Honey." Her voice went low. "I appreciate it, Lord knows I appreciate it more than I can even say, but you know I can't."

"You can," he said simply. "You deserve to be happy." What he didn't add was *you deserve to be free—like me.*

Even in his thoughts, though, he was a hypocrite. He

could believe he was free all he wanted, but the pounding in his head told a different story.

He heard her breath on the line as she took a sip of what he knew was peppermint tea, and there were crickets behind her. She was on the porch, or in her new garden touching one of the petals on the rose bushes she was so proud of. It made him think of Val, the smell of her perfume.

"You know I appreciate whatever strength I was able to give you that got you away from him, but I'm not you. I chose this life, and divorce is not an option."

Her excuse, her forever excuse: the church wouldn't let her leave.

"He cheats on you." It was the freshest offense in his mind.

"Not anymore," she said. "You know he doesn't do any of the things he did anymore. He's changed, Alec. I wish you'd come here and see."

"Right," he managed. It didn't seem coincidental that things got better for his mom once he was gone. Maybe he'd bought her the house just so he could have a home where he could feel welcome again.

This was where the conversation always dripped down to. That his father had changed. Gone to God—the God who wouldn't let his mother divorce him—and had all the dickhead sucked out. For his mother's sake, he hoped it was true. He hadn't seen his father in ten years, since he took off for New York City.

He'd hated leaving his mom that day. This had been his way to finally make up for it. He knew one day he would save her.

Why won't she let me?

His mother might have been the only woman in the world he couldn't get to do what he wanted. The irony was not lost on him.

"How can you forgive him?" he finally said. It wasn't the question he wanted to ask. He wanted to ask: *How could you have stayed? If you knew how messed up I would be now, would you have stayed for eighteen years when he didn't have a God at all? When that same God didn't save you?*

"Forgiving him is all I have," she said.

"Bye, Mom." He needed to end this conversation.

"Bye, bye, honey, and don't forget to tell Val I said hi."

Alec clicked off his phone and shoved it in his pocket. *Val*. Alec took a long drink of his beer. She'd been the only thing in his life that made sense. He kept scolding himself for fucking up the calm sailboat of their relationship, but damn the rocking had been fun—the capsizing into the water, the splashing around. So much so that he'd forgotten about the house again until that stupid moment with Randy Tines.

A little more rocking might be just what he needed to put this crap out of his mind for a while. Unfortunately he'd come to the end of that road. Val had made that clear. He really thought she might take him into her mouth—well, the Val she used to be never would, but there was a side to her he'd never known. A side he realized now, he might never get out of his system.

Chapter Eleven

When she didn't find Alec at the bar, the bartender pointed Valerie in the direction of the pinball room at the back of the arcade.

He played at a machine directly across the room from the open door. Neon light and computerized music splashed against the wood-paneled walls as he pushed the flipper buttons. It provided the perfect cover to stare at him without interruption. His strong arms gripped the sides of the machine. The back of his head was a sexy mess of brown hair. Valerie knew his eyes were filled with the determined stare they got when he was concentrating, that his jaw was taut and sure. He seemed to pump against it as he kept the ball zipping and pinging, his ass clenched as he…

"If you want a show," Alec said, not turning around, "all you have to do is ask, Val."

Busted. Her face boiled; her stomach became a hard knot. She was not nearly sly enough to tango with the likes of Alec. She tamped down her silly humiliation. There was absolutely nothing wrong with appreciating a man's fine ass.

But this wasn't just any man, this was Alec.

"I'm not interested in the kind of show you're used to giving." Her voice was light, but her heart was at the apex of her throat.

"I know," he said quietly. "We're all done with that."

Logically she knew they should be. So why could she not stop thinking about finishing what she'd started earlier? What he'd told her he wanted. Maybe that really was all she needed to do to be over him. Maybe things felt weird because she'd had two orgasms and he'd only had one. They were imbalanced. Once they were even she could let the desire go.

What the hell am I doing? Having a sexual trial in my mind? One thing was for sure, they were both innocent and both ferociously guilty.

"You weren't at the bar." She made her way across the floor. The click of her heels against the smooth wood laminate fought against the machines pinging around her.

"Yeah, the local news was at the window, so they let me come back here."

"Who called them?" Her focus switched to Alec's comment. Chronic Disharmony might be on hiatus, but the media never was.

"Who knows?" His voice was stiff. "This was the one place I thought I could trust people. I should know there are assholes everywhere."

She was surprised Alec was willing to trust anyone. He'd never told her that he couldn't, exactly, but she knew that wariness was from where so many of his choices stemmed. Not knowing what the word *trust* really meant.

It was why he couldn't be the guy who cuddled and murmured into her hair, why he'd never be the man waiting for her in a tuxedo at the end of an aisle, but for the moment maybe he didn't have to be. He thought she gave a *fucking amazing blowjob*. His words still sizzled in her brain.

"Hopefully they didn't ruin your night," she said, the sexual timbre of her voice surprising her.

"I have a private pinball room. My night couldn't be going too much better." He pulled the lever and sent another ball flying.

"It couldn't?"

Seriously, what are you doing?

"Oh, it could," he replied, "but the rest of this weekend will be filled with PG fun only. Dr. Barkin's orders. Want to play?"

Was that what she really wanted, PG fun only?

She peeked at his ass again, pictured it braced against the machine as her mouth and tongue pleasured him beyond his imagination. Her resolve rose with her desire. Before she could stop it, a whimper escaped her throat and a drip defied her between her legs.

"My very own pinball room," he mused. "Who knew it would take getting famous to live the dream I had when I was fifteen?"

There was no doubt she wanted him. But could she really be the hunter? And now that she had her prey cornered, what was she supposed to do? She wasn't used to making the first move, and she definitely wasn't used to it with someone who had seen every first move ever invented.

"Valcrie, do you want to play?"

Maybe he hadn't meant his words as innuendo, but in that moment, she couldn't take them any other way.

She stepped closer to him. Her stomach was a whisper away, her breasts a sigh away. So close. Surges of heat fired at her from his back. He could probably hear her heart thrumming as she reached out her hand, her finger paused a gasp away from his waist.

She inhaled and closed her eyes. They had done this already. It was not difficult: *trace your fingers along his shoulder, murmur into his ear, spin him around, kneel down in front of him, unbuckle his belt, and take him into your eager mouth.*

Easy.

Simple.

Her stomach was a seesaw winging up and down.

She needed to stop thinking. She needed to do. She'd spent most of her life on pause. Except for her music, she never went after what she wanted. She never demanded it. That was changing this very minute.

She snaked her hand around his side, fingertips leading the way. "Was that the only dream you had at fifteen?" She slid her hand onto his rock-hard stomach. *Crap, does he mine diamonds in there?*

He tensed, then relaxed as her fingers splayed along his abdominal muscles. Her pinky grazed his belt buckle. It was ice cold from the air conditioning.

"Definitely not." His breath was a heavy moan when he turned to face her. He slipped his hands around her waist and pulled her to him in one quick motion, his eyes filled with hunger.

She inhaled sharply. She couldn't ignore the shock wave when his hardest parts banked up against her softest ones. But this was her seduction, and while she wanted whatever he was about to offer her, she wanted to give him what she'd planned all the more.

She stepped back and rolled her fingers down his chest, the tips of them studying every rock, every crevasse. She breathed out and gathered more courage. "Was one of them getting your dick sucked in an arcade?"

Those words would have usually stayed in her mind flipping somersaults. She stopped breathing until Alec's eyes went dark, and his erection pulsed against her thigh.

"At fifteen my dreams didn't go that far," he admitted.

"This very minute, though…" He took a finger and slid it along her lips. "It's at the top of my list."

She took his finger in her mouth, worked it in and out. Her tongue slicked around it, giving him a preview of what she was planning. She was woozy for what was under that belt buckle.

His breath caught. He dipped her chin back, forcing her to let go, even as their heartbeats fought against the arcade's sounds.

"Val." His eyes darted like pinballs as they grazed over her face. "What about your rules?"

Crap, maybe she couldn't just do. Maybe all her thinking and pausing earlier would make just doing impossible.

"Do you want me to stop?" She deposited her hand where it had been, palm open, wrist tight against his waistband, her pinky sliding underneath to hot skin.

"Fuck no," he breathed. "You can feel how hard I am for you. I just want to make sure this is okay."

She moved slowly toward the door to close it, hoping to increase his ache with each swing of her hips. "That's how sure I am," she said, more seriously than she'd intended as she made her way back over to him, "but right now I don't need you to be a gentleman. I need you to pull my hair while I take you into my mouth, and I need you to come at the back of my throat." Her heart was beating like the midnight cheep of a cuckoo clock, but she kept her words steady. "Do you think you can do that?"

She'd never spoken to a man this way, and the words excited her. Lust flowered in her abdomen and tumbled lower. Alec appraised her again. Each sweep of his gaze garnered an additional heartbeat and an additional thrum of need.

"Dirty Girl," he finally said, straddling the legs of his jeans wide, "none of that is going to be a problem."

She eased her hand into his waistband. He was so hard

already, his skin smooth and hot.

No more thinking.

She lowered his pants and boxers, angling him so his ass butted against the front of the pinball machine. She dropped to her knees, her lips a tongue's length away from him. She breathed in his scent, his heat. Her eyes feasted on his panty-scorching length. He was thick and long, smooth and pulsing.

She laid small kisses along his hip bones, and he answered her with a sigh. She licked at the inside of his thighs, at the base of him, putting her mouth everywhere but where she'd promised.

His breath exploded like a boiling tea kettle. "Fuck, I need to be inside that mouth."

She snaked her hands up and darted them down the front of his thighs. "I know how much you enjoy teasing." She gave him a wry smile. She knew her lips were wet and swollen from her preview. Knew he was coveting them, craving them.

His fingers urged at the base of her skull. "I'm going to regret that, aren't I?"

"You have no idea." She fisted him at the base and slicked her hand over him so slowly that he'd feel each ridge of her fingertips. She brought her mouth closer and hot breath banked back on her chin. Her lower lip teased against the softest, most sensitive part of him and he groaned. She opened her mouth a click, giving him a taste of what was in store, and he growled.

He jerked back. "Get those elegant flute-player lips around my cock before I come all over your face, before it's dripping down your chin and neck."

"Patience." She sighed, an army of goose bumps marching beneath the heat of her breath.

His voice originated from a low hiss. "I fucking love your sexy voice almost as much as I love your blowjobs, but right now I only want that mouth working on one thing—my cock."

"I know exactly what you want." She reveled in the power. Alec was completely under her spell. When she was with him like this, she was the sexy, confident woman he believed she was. When she was about to give him pleasure, she could accept all his compliments. The control made her hotter than any touch, wetter than any lick. Damp fever seeped from the summit of her thighs.

Could she orgasm from giving *him* a blowjob?

She dove back in, looping her tongue around his tip but keeping the whole of her mouth back, pumping him with her hand.

"Seriously"—he gasped—"me fucking your mouth, now."

She obliged, slowly gliding him between her lips, slicking the top of his shaft with her tongue. She'd learned earlier he was too large to take in all at once.

He moaned his approval. "Fuck, Dirty Girl, you suck that cock like you've been playing it all your life."

His words forced her to take him deeper, deeper, so he strained the back of her throat. She sucked and slicked and slid her hand over him for a good two minutes before she had to pause.

"One breath, and then I want that swallow you promised. I want to come hot and thick into that wicked mouth."

She inhaled like she was going under water and slicked her lips faster around his length. He rocked and jerked into her mouth. His pursuit of pleasure made her moan and hum into his skin.

"Fuck," he gasped. He braced himself, and she tasted the first hint of salt. He was about to come. She opened her throat, swallowing around him as his orgasm boiled out. He shrieked with pleasure as she accepted every last bit of him.

She wiped her mouth. His breathing was heavy, his pupils pinpricks. The look in his eyes was as unrelenting as an erupting volcano as he reached his hand out and lifted her to her feet.

He pulled her into his chest. "I think you've ruined me."

She smiled against his shoulder.

His lips hovered on her forehead, his stubble grating her skin. "No," he murmured. "I know you have."

"I'll ruin you anytime." She welcomed his arms and lips and sank deeper, until her mind flipped on and she stepped back. He seemed confused, before the reminder must have hit him, too. *This is just sex. We are just sex.*

"Here." He coughed, handing her his beer.

She took a long drink, but the taste of him was still on her lips. They stood next to each other, catching their breath and probably their thoughts. The ones she was running after: *Why am I still thinking about him? That was supposed to have cured us both.*

Valerie's face, her whole body, was on fire; she squeezed her legs together but the friction just stoked the flames. She wanted Alec again, on her, in her. She'd thought that would get him out of her system. She'd been wrong. If they stayed this close she was going to jump him.

I'll ruin you anytime. Those words were not in line with her rules.

She made her way to the closest pinball machine in playing distance. Something called *Shaq Attack*. Basketball and arcade games, two of her least favorite things, but anything was better than losing herself in Alec again.

"You got a quarter?" she asked.

"That game sucks."

She bit her lip and managed a tight laugh.

"Crap, you know what I mean," he said as he handed her a coin.

She tried to play, but she couldn't stop thinking about Alec—couldn't stop seeing his strained face as he orgasmed in the flashing lights, his dick in the flippers at the bottom of the machine. She needed to change the subject. But her mind was blank. Even when he was talking about a dumb pinball game, she'd equated it to their latest sexual encounter.

All their sexual encounters had turned this man beside her from Alec into a man who made her senseless with want. He was her best friend in name only.

Reece's annoying screech traveled in from the hallway behind the closed door.

Valerie's body tensed. The ball fell in a perfect line down the length of the machine and into the hole between the flippers. "I cannot take any more of her tonight."

Alec rushed to the closed door and locked it. "She might have a voice that can break glass, but she's not getting in here without a key."

Recce's nails-against-a-chalkboard tone continued to strike above the sound of the pinball machines. Valerie shook her head in disapproval. "Can you imagine when she has kids?"

"Oh…" Alec touched his chin. "My mom says hi."

"Oh my God!" Val shrieked. "You have got to stop it with that."

"Sorry, bad joke," he admitted. He shoved his hands into his pockets. "It's really true, though. I just talked to her."

Val calmed her initial tension. Recurring odd timing for his mom's salutation or not, she was glad for the distraction. Something she and Alec could talk about that wouldn't lead to their hands all over each other.

"How is she?"

"Still eating shit as fast as my dad can shovel it."

"I'm sorry." Val's voice broke. She never knew how to talk to Alec about his family, but she knew how to listen, so she did.

"I just don't understand why she's still with him." Pain pierced his eyes.

She knew there was something he wasn't saying. She let him not say it.

His mouth tightened. "You know all this. You've heard it before." He pressed a hand to the back of his head and winced.

Valerie touched his other hand, trying to bring him back to her. "I'll hear it again."

Her touch was supposed to be innocent. A way to say *I'm here for you*, like she always had been, like she always would be, but the fever coming from Alec let her know that innocent would never be a category in their relationship again. She couldn't help rolling her fingertips in small circles over his knuckles, and her breath escalated, betraying her further.

Alec's eyes heated and darkened to deep brown, turning almost black. Without a word, he picked her up, spun her around, and laid her on top of the pinball machine.

"What are you doing?" she asked, even though she knew—even though she wanted it.

He wound a hand up her thigh, rousing the simmer between her legs that she'd failed to extinguish. "It's my turn, Dirty Girl."

She waited, breathless, his next move her only oxygen.

He stood above her and straddled his arms along her thighs. "I need you to claw at my hair while I slick your sweet clit with my tongue, and I need you to come all over my lips. Do you think you can do that?"

He'd mirrored her words. How could she say no? She nodded.

His voice was gravel. "Spread your legs."

She lay back and followed his instruction. His fingers found the waistband of her panties, and he tugged them down. He squeezed them in his hand. "You didn't tell me how wet you were."

His words brought a pulse from where she needed to be

touched, to be claimed. He stuck his head under her skirt, positioned himself between her legs, and licked his way up the contours of her thighs. Her body convulsed, called out to him as he got closer.

"Sucking my cock got you all worked up, didn't it?"

"Yes." She angled her hips up, begging for the firmness of his lips.

"That mouth I just fucked, I'm going to make it scream until it's raw. What do you think about that?"

"Yes," she repeated. It was the only word in her mind, huge and neon-bright.

"Say it. Tell me you want me to fuck you with my tongue."

She managed a raspy breath. She wanted even more than what he was ordering, and she was going to demand it. "I want you to annihilate me with your tongue."

He pulled back to look at her, his eyes laser sharp, his lips shiny and about to be hers. "Lucky for you, I never leave a lady unsatisfied."

As the first glide of his tongue hit what had been swollen and ready for him, she knew she'd never heard a truer statement.

Chapter Twelve

"You do know they have breakfast for us at the hotel?" Val asked as they walked down the dairy aisle of Wegmans.

Instead of attending Reece's itinerary-mandated breakfast, or even getting room service, Alec had brought her to buy groceries at the store where they both had summer jobs during high school. It was no coincidence. He could have picked any one of the stores Kenmore had to offer, but he'd wanted to be with Valerie in a place they both knew well.

If he had to do something he was dreading, he'd comingle it with memories. He pulled his baseball cap down and adjusted his sunglasses.

Alec searched through the cheese. "Do you work for Reece now or what?"

Val threw back her head and released a throaty laugh. "Of course not, I'm just wondering why you're buying"—she glanced into his basket—"orange juice, eggs, bread—"

"Don't forget sharp cheddar," he interrupted, tossing it in. He continued down the aisle and added milk and creamer, too. "Coffee, then we're done."

Her big brown eyes examined Alec's face, or what she could see of it under his "disguise." She'd always indulged his impish side, but he knew she was definitely curious. Downright desperate to know where they were going.

He couldn't tell her yet, because he still wasn't sure he'd have the courage to drive to the house he'd bought for his mother. To see it still empty—to finally accept it would be forever.

That word, that fucking word, kept mocking him.

Last night with Valerie had been incredible, but they'd still somehow stood firm on her basic rules. The rules he now saw made sense. The rules he was thankful for. They were the only thing keeping him tethered in reality. Reminding him that one day from now, Valerie went back to Philly and he went back to L.A. and they went back to being best friends and nothing more.

Val cocked her head. "Where do you plan on making all this? On the hood of the Maserati?"

"You'll see." It was too much to explain here, too much to explain now.

After grabbing the coffee, they headed toward the cash register. When they slid past the produce department, a memory hit him hard, as if one of the coconuts stacked up had knocked him in the head.

He stopped in front of the precarious pyramid of brown wooden balls. "Remember when we both called in sick the summer of senior year to go to the Coldplay concert?"

Valerie was in tiny khaki shorts and a tight navy blue T-shirt. Her sneakers squeaked on the shiny grocery store floor. "How could I forget?" Her lips eased into a smile as the memory hit her, too.

He'd loved that day. It was them, only them. They'd traveled by bus to New York City. He said he was sleeping at Gideon's. She said she was sleeping at Cynthia's. The lie, all the lies, had been easy for him, but Val had struggled. She didn't lie to her parents, not intentionally, but she'd made an exception for music, for him.

"That was when you decided to move to New York after high school," she said, looking down.

She probably hadn't meant to bring it up. He certainly hadn't expected her to. They hadn't ever talked about the day she said no. He wondered if she thought about it as much as he did, or if only the memory had brought her back there.

After graduation, up until the last minute before he left, even up until the train conductor closed the doors, he'd thought she'd join him. That was the thing that was hardest for him to admit, that even after she said no, he still believed she would change her mind.

"You made the right decision that day." The words came out before he could stop them. It was as much the truth as it was a lie.

She pursed her lips, like she was trying to hide that his words had stung her. "I still feel bad about it, though."

"Why? We were kids," he said, trying to play it off.

He appreciated her remorse now, but he'd needed her kindness then. Needed understanding instead of the frown she offered at his plea, needed joy instead of the look of fear in her eyes at his insistence that they could do anything as long as they were together.

"You were never a kid, Alec."

"Neither were you, Val."

"I just wish…" A muscle quivered in her jaw, but she didn't continue. Perhaps she was wondering the same things he was. If she had come, would they be more than friends now? More than whatever this weekend was molding them into and what the end of it would mold them out of?

She would never reply, *I should have thrown away my future on a boy who at the time didn't have one, just had a guitar and a dream.* It was probably part of the reason she'd made her rules—she knew he was a man still carrying that boy.

So why couldn't he help wondering? He might deny himself her flesh going forward, but she had burrowed into his brain nice and tight.

"You knew you couldn't count on me." He shrugged. "I don't blame you for that."

He didn't, not anymore. Perhaps she had been as much his friend that day as ever, looking out for him like she always had. He'd tried to go too far too fast. He hadn't been ready for what he was really asking for, and she knew it.

"Thank you," she replied. "I guess we were just too young."

If they were too young then, what were they now?

He nodded. "We're older, but clearly you still can't count on me. I was four hours late to meet you this weekend."

"I can count on you for some things, Alec."

Yeah, the things he could offer from three thousand miles away. What he'd asked for ten years ago, what he knew she wanted from a man today, was a whole different level of significance. Something he shouldn't have been playing with then; something he couldn't believe he was playing with now.

"You don't have to be sorry for knowing me better than I knew myself."

She averted her eyes. "I am, but apology officially rescinded, then," she finally said. She exhaled, seemed to gather herself, before she spoke again. "But I didn't even know you could cook."

Her words magically turned the cement in his chest into floating motes of ivory dust, and he could breathe again. Val always knew when he was getting in too deep.

He couldn't cook, but how hard could it be to make stupid eggs?

"I think, this weekend, we've discovered there's a lot you don't know about me." He couldn't help inching closer to her even in the middle of the produce aisle, near enough he could smell every petal in her perfume. "And a whole lot more I don't know about you."

He was hoping to avoid this. But maybe there was no avoiding it. Maybe whenever they were together their bodies would take them here, rules or not.

Val's eyes blazed, but he stepped back. He was about to let the moment go when she added, "And just think of everything you have left to learn."

He banked his gaze right up against the fire of her eyes. "When you talk to me that way, it makes me think you want to show me right now."

Her lips parted. "We should probably eat first."

"First?" Did that mean she wanted to do something after? Fuck, he wanted to kiss the crap out of those lips. He wanted to do whatever she would allow him to. He knew it wasn't smart, but his cock was no Einstein, never had been.

"I just mean breakfast is the most important m-meal of the day," she stammered, trying to save herself—trying to save them both.

He could have just led her over to the registers and let it go, but his cock spoke before he could stop it. "Thinking you'll need your energy for something?"

...

Somehow, they made it out of Wegmans without Alec being recognized or screwing her against the coconut pyramid. Yes, she'd pictured Alec dropping his basket, sending creamer and coffee and oranges airborne, and then he was on her, angling her body against whatever he could find. Her ass knocking into the coconuts, forcing them to roll like marbles all over the floor as he ripped off her shorts right in the middle of the store.

She harnessed the mustang canter of her heart as she awakened from her fantasy and remembered they were in the Maserati with the top down. The wind whipped at her skin and in her hair. She also couldn't believe they'd talked about New York. While she truly was sorry, she was thankful he'd reminded her of the one thing she kept forgetting: *you can't count on me.*

She was fooling herself if she thought Alec was any different than he was that day ten years ago. But he'd never promised to be; she needed to remember that, too.

She'd checked her phone already that morning, but she looked at her inbox once again and found nothing from London. She really should have heard by now, so maybe the answer was no. She glanced at Alec, adding yet another reason to keep her feelings contained to the mounting list. She could only take so much rejection this weekend.

But why was she wrapping them together? London and Alec were separate parts of her life, or at least they had been until the past forty-eight hours when she started to wonder if Alec wanted to be her whole life.

She still wasn't sure where they were going. They rode down the familiar streets of Kenmore, past the neighborhood where she grew up and beyond, to one of the swankiest areas of town. An etched wood sign with stone accents that read SHERIDAN ESTATES announced their location.

Her parents' house had been upper-middle-class nice. Way nicer than Alec's, he always pointed out, but nowhere close to as ritzy as this street. The kids who attended private schools lived in this neighborhood. It was where everyone in town went on Halloween to trick or treat and catch glimpses of houses they could never dream of owning.

"I'm still totally confused," Val said, trying to get Alec to spill. He was in a variation of his rock star uniform, dark jeans, black boots, a matching leather belt, and a tight black T-shirt.

According to Reece's itinerary, they were supposed to go hiking and swimming today. Not that he'd ever seemed to care, but he was not dressed for it. The bikini bottom she wore under her shorts was riding up. Why did she need to be prepared for everything all the time? She wished she could be a little more like Alec.

They turned down Niagara Street and pulled into a circular driveway. A beautiful, newly constructed red brick colonial with a wedding-cake-frosting white door sat tall and fat in the center.

"Here we are." Alec took a deep breath and exited the car.

Val stared at the house; it was magnificent, though the lawn and landscaping were overgrown and mail and papers were piled like snow drifts beside the door.

What are we doing here? Are we going to break in?

"Are you coming?" He was already standing on the gray-white concrete porch with the groceries, kicking the mail to the side, his sunglasses off, his hat in the back pocket of his jeans.

Though she was still unsure, she exited the car and joined him. "Whose house is this?" She tried to make out a name on one of the pieces of mail, but he gripped her wrist, stopping her. "Does it matter?"

He bent down and grabbed a single key from one of the fake rock hiding places advertised in the airplane magazine she'd actually perused in an attempt to stop looking at *Rolling Stone*.

She guessed they weren't breaking in.

The door creaked as he opened it. She stepped in behind him. The foyer was done in huge marble tiles. A gigantic oak staircase and high ceilings reached up to the second floor.

"Whose house is this?" she repeated.

"Please stop asking." He gave her a firm look. "I need some coffee and food before I can get into all that."

All that? Where the hell are we?

He began to move through the foyer, but she stood tentatively. Her curiosity and uncertainty would not allow her to follow.

"Val." Alec pulled the grocery bag up on one arm and squeezed his hand around hers. "I promise we are allowed to be here. No silent alarm has been tripped. No police are on the way." He met her eyes. "Okay?"

His brown eyes were filled with assurance, and their hands locked tight confirmed it. Nothing had ever been more okay. She nodded and allowed him to lead her farther into the house.

The kitchen was similarly stunning, outfitted with granite countertops, stainless steel appliances, a long wood and glass dining table, and warm wood floors. Though the window above the sink had a baseball-size hole in it, like a rock had been thrown through.

"Sit." He indicated one of the stools at the bar lining the center island, ignoring the window.

She deposited herself in the seat closest to the stove as he emptied the groceries onto the counter and started coffee brewing. He opened one of the lustrous wood cabinets—it was filled with dishes. He opened the next, filled with glasses. The next, filled with small appliances. He didn't stop until he found the one containing pots and pans and took out a skillet.

Wherever they were, he hadn't been here before.

He put the skillet on the stove and poured her a steaming cup of coffee, deposited cream and the cup in front of her.

"How do you like your eggs?" His eyes were so tight on her she thought she might crack in half. Something about the way he asked, the way he watched her pour cream into her coffee, told her he cared far more about her answer than he should.

"Scrambled," she said.

A wistful smile streaked his lips. "Me too." He looked at the eggs on the counter. Opened the package and looked at them some more.

"Do you need any help?"

Alec shook his head. He set his jaw and lifted his chin. His determination was beyond endearing.

"Why don't I grab a bowl?" she suggested, giving him a bit of direction.

He'd never admit he needed help, even when it came to something as basic as scrambled eggs. She slid off the stool and headed over to the cabinet filled with cookware, took out a mixing bowl, and grabbed a whisk out of the utensil cup.

She placed them on the counter next to him. "Crack away, Julia Child."

Alec took out an egg and studied it. "Can you think of a male chef's name to call me? I can't deal with you picturing me as a chubby French woman all morning."

"Why's that?" Val asked with a gentle laugh.

Alec shot her a knowing smile, an *I've been inside you and had you in my mouth* smile.

The kind that had only surfaced this weekend. She attempted to drag in a steady breath, but all her body's attention had been sucked between her thighs.

Focus on the conversation, Val, focus on the conversation. "Do you seriously care what I call you?"

"Nicknames are important," he replied, cracking an egg into the bowl. He turned to the stove and flipped the burner on under the skillet. "I think you know that better than anyone," he said, tossing a pat of butter in the pan, "Dirty Girl."

The sizzle mimicked the hiss in Valerie's belly. Hearing her nickname on his lips sent her spiraling. Made her want to act like the hot, sexy, naughty temptress he believed she was. She steadied herself against the counter, her fingers shuddering to touch him, her body humming like a harmonica, deep and low.

He'd hypnotized her. Those words were like her marching orders now.

She gathered up the sexual strength they gave her. "I earned that nickname."

He turned to her, his eyes as explosive as lightning.

She forced herself to stare deep and continued. "When I taste the breakfast you made, we'll see what nickname you get."

He quirked an eyebrow. "Bring it on."

Potent silence hung between them while he finished cracking the eggs. He turned back to the stove, his ass in dark jeans on display for her as he poured the eggs into the pan. A bit splashed up on him and he stepped back.

"You need an apron, Julia?" She smiled, unable to help herself.

She waited for him to come back with a similar quip, but she was underestimating him. She should have learned that by now.

He removed his shirt and lay it on the barstool. "An apron won't be necessary."

Holy Cock-fucius.

Alec shirtless, at the stove with the morning light hitting his broad back, the muscles of his shoulders, was almost too much. His brown hair was matted from his baseball hat, the skin of his neck pink from concentration. He might not know it, but he was creating the morning after of her dreams.

His tattoos seemed to breathe as he worked—the wing of feathers flapping and flying, the vine of thorns growing like ivy. The boiling coffee in her hand was at a lower temperature than her body. She took a long sip of it in an attempt to cool down. "I'm pretty sure that's a health code violation." She was trying to keep her words measured, but she was beyond tempted to walk up behind him, turn off the stove, and screw him against it.

"I think you'll be calling the health department anyway, once you taste *these*." He indicated the pan.

She pushed herself up on the stool to get a better look. They were the ugliest scrambled eggs she'd ever seen, but because he was making them for her, she couldn't wait to eat them.

He took the eggs off the stove and served them up on two plates, depositing soggy toast beside them. "Wow," he said, shaking his head, "who fucks up toast?"

She laughed at his statement, gaped at his still shirtless chest. Had his muscles gotten tauter overnight, his abs more defined? "I'm sure it will taste delicious."

I'm hungry, all right.

She herded her disobedient eyes to her plate. There was only one dish on the menu that morning.

He took a seat across from her and they ate in silence — the ting of forks, the slurp of coffee, the non-crunch of his toast. It was not gourmet, but they both ate greedily. She wasn't sure if it was out of hunger or out of uncertainty.

They'd had plenty of silences in their relationship, but it was not lost on her that this silence was new, expectant.

She bit her lip; she shouldn't be expecting anything. Certainly not what all their flirting this morning would lead to if they were a normal couple. The reminder knocked against her brain — *we are not a normal couple.*

"How come we're not talking?" she finally asked.

Alec's gaze intensified. "We can talk. What do you want to talk about?"

"I don't know," she blurted, more harshly than she'd intended. "I feel like..." She swallowed, searching for words.

"I can't tell you things the way I used to. Or at least, I think about everything I'm going to say before I say it."

He fisted a light punch against her chin. "In your case that might not be a bad thing."

She glanced down, unable to look him in the eye. He wasn't taking this seriously. He wasn't taking her seriously—yet another reminder to add to the list.

"Val." He reached out for her hand, forced her to look at him. His eyes were like caramel in the sunlight. "Nothing has changed. We're still exactly the same. I can tell you anything, and you can tell me anything."

She paused, uncertainty scratching at her belly.

"Tell me something," he pushed.

She exhaled. This was her chance. He was asking, for God's sake. *I'm having confusing feelings about you. I know I'm supposed to be able to compartmentalize sex and friendship, but both sides are overflowing and mixing together into one big beautiful mess.* No, she couldn't just say that. She needed him to speak, to prove that nothing had changed.

She jutted her chin out in determination. "You first."

"I can't cook," he admitted, his face spreading into a smile.

She returned it even though she knew he was still playing with her. "That's no secret." She allowed the two of them to spin in that carefree haze for only a moment before she gave him a heavy look that demanded more.

He blinked, ran his finger along the rim of his mug, and let out a jerky breath. He was going to tell her something big, something terrible. She braced herself, hoping to hell it wasn't about her, about them.

"This house"—he opened his hands to indicate the kitchen around him—"is my mother's."

Phew, not about her. But why was that huge news? Her face creased in confusion.

"I bought it for her," he explained, "so she could finally

leave my dad."

"Alec," Valerie said, her breath high in her throat, "that was so amazing of you. When is she moving in?"

"She doesn't want it," he admitted, his eyes dull. "She doesn't want to leave him."

Val's lungs felt like they had been popped, air shooting up and scratching her throat. "I'm sure if you just told her—"

He held his hand up. "No, it's been a year. I can't ask anymore." His voice was monotone.

He'd kept this secret from her for a year. She let it sink in, though she understood. There was nothing more embarrassing and hurtful than being rejected by your own mother.

"I'm so sorry." She knew this was about more than the house. It was Alec trying to save his mother, to do what he couldn't do as a teenager or a child. He'd admitted a long time ago that his helplessness in the face of his father was his biggest regret.

The paleness that bathed his face pushed her to speak again, suddenly desperate to do anything to wash away his pain. "This isn't your life anymore, Alec, and maybe your mom knows it. She's allowing you to leave this behind."

"I thought I'd escaped. I realize now he's right here." He pressed his hand to his temple. "Maybe he always will be."

His words, his admission, were pulling her face closer—to his cheek, to his jaw, to his lips. Her pulse banged at her neck. She was going to kiss him. He was going to kiss her.

No, she couldn't—as much as she wanted to, she couldn't. Once she broke that rule, the confusion would have nowhere left to go but straight to the center of her heart. She somehow managed to pull back.

"There's one other thing." Alec reached for her hand and laced his fingers with hers. "I just realized that this attempt at breakfast, at food…" He chuckled. "It wasn't just about eating or even an excuse to bring you here."

The stiffness she hadn't realized she was holding in her shoulders fell.

His chin was in a persistent line. "When we were in high school, do you remember how I snuck in and stayed over sometimes?"

She nodded, spooling back to the memory. He'd come to her first-floor bedroom window late at night, eyes wet and frightened. He would take his place on her floor, she on her bed, and they would stare at the glow-in-the-dark stars on her ceiling, talking about the future. The lives they could have beyond the walls of their parents' houses, beyond their stupid town.

It was ironic that a future they'd never even considered, that Val still wasn't sure of, had brought them right back here—right back into one of their parents' houses.

"I'd always have to leave when your mom started making breakfast. The smell of coffee was my cue to go," he said, "my signal refuge was over."

"Alec," she managed. Her throat was tight, and warmth welled up in her—a fountain of emotion.

He scrubbed a hand over his face. "I might not have realized it until you were sitting across from me in the sun, but having a time where I could have breakfast with you, Val, just once, just the two of us—one time when my refuge didn't have to end is the only thing that matters right now."

Her heart seemed to swing like a pendulum; the warmth that had started low deluged her chest and every limb, like she was a maple tree filled with sweet, gooey sap.

She was kissing him *now*. Screw her stupid rules. They couldn't stop her from this feeling, from this want. From responding to the sweet gesture he'd offered her that morning. She leaned in to him, slowly at first, so he'd know exactly where she was going—for his lips, his sweet, hot, naughty lips.

She brushed against them lightly, testing, but when Alec

pressed against her with more force, opened her mouth with his tongue and dove in deep, she could do nothing but meet his demand—nothing but ride to wherever he was taking her.

・・・

Kissing Valerie. *I am kissing Valerie*—her soft lips, her expert tongue.

It wasn't where he'd expected this morning to go, but he was finally tasting her, all of her. He drove his lips against hers, their tongues glided and wound, until the kiss became hungry, until the innocent, testing lips they had started with were overwhelmed by their want. Their kiss continued to build, expanding and spiraling down to his cock where the need for her detonated, turned his body to ragged ash.

His lips were unrelenting as his hands cut from her face, down her neck, to cup her tits. His fingers traced over them lightly, as if their first kiss made this new—like they were discovering each other for the first time.

She whimpered under his touch, and he fought the urge to travel beneath her shirt. He wanted this. Holy fucking shit, did he want this, but he needed to hear that she did, too.

Their bodies never said no. Their bodies couldn't be trusted.

He put his hand to the side of her face, her skin hot and shiny. "If we keep going, I'm going to have to have you naked and panting under me."

"I know." She scanned his face. Her eyelashes flitted like butterflies around her big brown eyes.

"I'm not going to break your rules unless you tell me to."

"You kissed me back," she said with a sly smile. "That was a rule."

"I couldn't not kiss you back, Val. I couldn't not kiss you," he admitted. Their bodies were still so close. The skin of his bare chest itched to be against hers.

"Me neither." Her mouth parted. A mouth he still had the taste of, was still desperate to taste.

He ran his thumb along her jaw. "Truth is, now that you have kissed me, I'm never going to be able to follow that rule again."

Could their screwing turn sweet like this? In some ways it was what he wanted. To kiss every uncharted inch of her, take his time with her pleasure rather than fuck her hard and fast, but he knew how dangerous that was. If he felt like this after one kiss, how would he feel after making love to her? And fuck, God help him, he wanted to.

But he would take her lead. See if she wanted him, or *all* of him.

She swallowed and he inched closer. "Say the words." He pressed his cheek to hers, his voice hungry.

"I-I want," she stammered. "I want you to fuck me." She slid her hand over his suddenly insanely hard cock.

Question answered. She wanted a fuck. What did he expect? He hadn't given her a ring—he'd made her breakfast, and he'd told her a secret. While both felt sweet and special to him, neither one was enough to warrant what he couldn't believe his heart seemed to be asking for.

"Then that's what you'll get, Dirty Girl." He lifted her from the stool and led her into the adjoining living room, depositing her on the white leather sectional. Instead of kissing her again, he stepped back. Turning his mind off and his body on, he was going to give her what she'd asked for.

"Take off your clothes. I want you naked against leather."

She hesitated.

"You want me to fuck you. I want you naked, now." His eyes did not leave hers. "Seems an even exchange."

She lowered her head, but he could tell she was going to acquiesce. She removed her shirt first, her hair tousled in its wake, then her shorts. She stood in front of him in a navy bikini top and matching bottom. The color on her pale skin was like blue dynamite.

"We were supposed to swim at the lake later." She smiled her explanation.

"I know," he said. "I'm glad I got to see you in this before anyone else did." He stepped closer. "I'm fucking thrilled I get to see you out of it." His fingers swept along her bare stomach. "Hurry."

She brushed her hair up and unfastened the bikini top. Her tits popped free, perky and perfect in the morning light.

"I will never get over your tits." He sighed as his eyes took their fill. "Your fucking exquisite body. Show me more. Show me everything."

She slid her fingers down the taut skin of her waist, slipping her bikini bottom down and off her right foot in one quick motion.

His eyes ravaged her, thankful for the chance to look for as long as he liked. His gaze darted from her creamy shoulders, to her luscious tits, to the manicured patch of hair he couldn't wait to run his fingers through, to the sweet, wet pussy it accentuated. He was tempted to tell her to turn around so he could stare at her ass uninterrupted, but he knew his hands all over it would be even better.

"V—" he started, but caught himself. Though he wanted to whisper her name, her real name while she stood naked and willing in front of him, that was a line he would never be able to uncross. "Dirty Girl, you are spectacular."

Her skin flushed the softest pink. "It feels weird to have you studying me."

"Just me?" He twirled a tendril of her hair around his finger. "Or any man?"

Her mouth lifted in invitation.

"You deserve to be studied." He shifted even closer. "Admired, worshipped," he continued, his hands finally connecting with her skin. It was hot, hotter than he'd expected, but goose bumps multiplied below his fingers as they journeyed from her clavicle to her tits. He fingered her nipples, and her back arched.

"You look so hot when you do that," he whispered. "When you show me how bad you want it."

She blinked, her mouth tightening.

"Remember, Dirty Girl, you can tell me anything."

"I'm craving more than that," she admitted, her skin going pinker.

A bell tolled in his gut. *Oh damn*, so was he. "Lay back," he instructed.

...

She dropped to the couch and waited, so ready for him. He stood above her and wrestled out of his jeans. The pronounced muscles of his abdomen gleamed with a sheen of sweat and his tattoos seemed to sparkle in the sunshine. Her mind was buzzing and her body was annihilated before his first thrust. They'd done all that sober. She'd done and said all that sober.

But it was because of what Alec was doing to her. Lust might have started the fire between them, but everything he'd shared at breakfast and their first sweet, tentative kiss had ignited a coal burning low in her heart. Warmth burrowed deep into the one place where she wasn't supposed to feel anything.

Her rules, created to keep her safe, seemed as flimsy as the bikini Alec had gotten her out of. They were no match for him and no match for the woman she became when she was with him.

With him. The words scared her for how familiar they were starting to sound.

"No bathing suit for you?" she asked, indicating the pinstriped boxers left in the wake of his jeans.

He slipped them off. "I don't swim, I skinny dip."

He moved to the couch and lay on top of her, her softness drowning in his hardness. His body lashed against hers as he attacked with deep, numbing kisses. With every stroke of their lips, need knotted tighter and tighter, a rope twisting and pulling her insides tauter, until she was afraid they might break. The ember of warmth glowing in her heart slid all the way down to her toes.

She was thankful she didn't have to say the words lodged in her throat. She could kiss her feelings into him, lie with him against leather and not say what she should not at all be feeling.

"That was a stupid rule," he admitted with a gasp. He kissed her again, more intensely, showing her just how stupid. His lips claimed hers, kissing ten years into ten seconds.

The room went blurry and her focus became savage. She pressed herself into his thigh, desperate for any attention. She needed something to keep her from saying the words that filled her like smoke when his lips touched hers: *I want this, I want you, for more than this second, for more than this weekend.*

"I'm neglecting you, aren't I?" he purred, sliding his hand to the spot she'd been angling for. His finger circled her and she moaned. "That won't happen again."

She spread her legs wider, opening herself to him. It was what she wanted, what she needed, to be so full of him her only attention would be on the satisfaction he could provide.

"Do you want me to fuck you now, Dirty Girl?"

She had to root herself in the words, because without them she would get lost in him. Maybe she already had. "Yes, fuck me now," she breathed.

"Your shiny, wet pussy is telling me it can't wait to take me deep." He riffled around on the floor for his pants and produced a condom. He ripped at the wrapper and set his gaze back on her.

"Wait!" she exclaimed. An idea sparked. To be in control of her uncontrollable thoughts, perhaps she needed to be in control of him. "I want *you* naked against leather."

"Dirty Girl…" His smile curved to meet the suggestive angle of her body.

"Sit," she commanded, indicating the other end of the couch with her chin. Shivers fluttered on top of her goose bumps as she waited for his response.

His smile melted as he accepted her command and sat on the buttery leather completely naked, condom still in his hand.

She managed to keep her trembling in check as she sauntered down the length of the couch, grabbed the condom wrapper, opened it, and rolled it over the length of him. He was so hard, it made her shudder.

She clasped his shoulder and spread her fingers like the feathers of his wing tattoo. She straddled him. She was ready to fly higher and higher, further away from her mind and deeper into the realm of her body. The one place that was safe, the one place she could show him how much she wanted him. She ran her breasts along the skin of his face and her core against what was hard and ready for her. A fever thundered through every nerve ending.

"You're teasing me," he whispered into her hair as she continued to taunt him. "I need to be inside you," he murmured, his breath sizzling against her nipple, "now."

"You want to fuck me?" Her question rocked the purr between her legs into a hungry tiger. It was the only place that could scream for him, that could admit what her mind had finally come to. She wanted to be with Alec. With the one man she knew could not be kept. "Say the word."

"I want you to fuck me." His breath was tight and his body was completely under her command. "I want you to ride me like the dirty girl you are."

• • •

He was ready to enter her with the force of an earthquake, leaving her body shattered and ruined, a fracture of passion with his name in its wake. Finally, mercifully, she lowered onto his lap and eased him inside. She was tight and slick and slowly she found her rhythm, their rhythm. He was close to coming—discharging his whole being into her waiting pussy—this morning becoming too much. He forced himself to hold back, to wait for her, his Dirty Girl, his Val.

She rode him harder, deeper, his hands holding onto her ass for dear life, his mouth finding one of her nipples and sliding his tongue in insistent circles. Her breathing increased, her sighs soared into moans.

"I can't barely last five minutes with you when you're hungry like this. Come all over my cock, Dirty Girl, while I squeeze your sweet ass."

Unexpectedly, her lips went for his, supplying devouring kisses that matched the power of her thrusts. Her mouth lit him on fire almost as much as pounding her pussy. She jerked, her body convulsing around him as he knew her wave was about to burst. He tumbled down with her, let his orgasm start its burning, searing, orchestral rise. His cock punched deeper, deeper as the syrupy relief washed over him in a core-smashing surge.

She worked to catch her breath above him, sweat slicking her skin. He was a mirror below, laying small kisses against her shoulder, along her neck.

The only word in his mind was her name, *Valerie*, repeating fast and slow, loud and quiet, insistent and like a sigh. The only question: how would he ever be able to survive back in L.A. without her when this weekend was over?

Chapter Thirteen

Valerie and Alec rushed to the trailhead. Their classmates were clumped in varying states of disinterest as Reece stood in front of them listing off dos and don'ts for the hike. They were dressed like Val was in shorts, sneakers, and T-shirts. Reece's outfit included a fisherman's hat and a backpack.

Alec was back in his rock star uniform of jeans and a black T-shirt. Valerie couldn't decide if she preferred him like this, rugged, antagonistic, and indifferent, or naked. Who was she kidding? The answer was naked.

"She looks like Dora the Explorer," Alec said.

Val laughed, thankful to get the magnificent image of Alec's naked body out of her head, along with the echoes of the words she'd been trying to cover up with it. "She does, but at least she's more prepared than you. Doesn't your stylist ever let you show a little leg?"

He nudged in close, his lips inches from her lobe. "I save that for special occasions." There was no doubt what he meant by that.

He could go from having her laughing to having her

worked up and wet in one line—in one hot whisper against the sensitive skin of her ear. She managed a glance at the midnight blue lake beside the trail where they would picnic later and wished she could jump in now just to douse the flames licking at her thighs.

Alec had more than satiated her that morning, but she was realizing with Alec her need might never end. She was just about to respond in kind, when Reece trained her booming voice at them.

"Nice of you to finally join us," she yelled out above the heads of the rest of their classmates.

There were a few laughs.

"Are we late?" Alec asked, glancing at his naked wrist.

There were more than a few laughs.

Valerie beamed at Alec's small victory over Commander Reece. Of course, she should have known that people like Reece didn't tolerate back talk and hated being laughed at even more.

"Yes, actually, you are," Reece replied, her face as severe as a storm warning. She held up her cell, open to the clock app for everyone to see. "Twelve minutes to be exact," she added. "We were about to leave without you."

"Wouldn't that have been a shame," Valerie shot back softly, her voice low enough she thought only Alec could hear.

Reece smiled wider than necessary. "Quiet, Valerie, no one cared what you had to say back in high school and no one cares now."

The rest of her classmates all turned to look, waited to see how and if Valerie would respond. Her skin chilled and her throat burned. Reece had clearly not forgotten the way she used to taunt Valerie in high school and must have thought she deserved a public dose. Valerie had no response. How did you reply to a statement you believed to be true in the darkest parts of yourself? In the parts you prayed no one would keep prying open?

Seeing she had Val, that her long-ago-established Achilles' heel was still raw, Reece continued. "In fact, I think people care less now than they did then. At least then people cared enough to make fun of you."

There was a collective, *ooooh* as in *burn*, from her classmates.

Barking, someone whispered from behind her, or was it her imagination? It didn't matter; if Reece remembered, everyone did. The nickname she'd hated echoed through the pine trees above, shot back down like a bird attacking. It was so stupid. She should have been ten years beyond that nickname now.

But she wasn't. Alec might have brought out a different side of her, showed her she wasn't the same Valerie she had been, but Reece only fueled what she knew. She was the same dorky, knock-kneed, stringy-haired Valerie. No matter how many standing ovations she heard or times Alec called her *Dirty Girl* and blew her mind, she was still reduced to the way other people viewed her.

Maybe Alec saw her the same way. Maybe that was why he'd agreed to sleep with her once, so he never had to again. But he *had* done it again…

"I care," Alec announced, loud enough for everyone to hear. He stood up taller, a sliver of a feather from his tattoo visible as he spread his broad shoulders even wider. She wished she could fly away with him on that wing.

"Oh, isn't that a surprise," Reece cackled. "Maybe if Valerie fluttered her eyelashes and drooled at me all day long, I would, too."

Cynthia caught Valerie's eye. "Screw her," she mouthed.

"Do you have anything else to say?" Reece inquired with a smile as sharp as a knife, "or may I continue?"

"Please," Alec said.

Val bit back more fire in her throat. She'd hoped Alec would continue to come to her rescue, but that was silly. No matter what things were like when they were alone, no matter where her mind went since they'd kissed, they weren't together. They were just friends. Why did she have to keep reminding herself?

"Okay, thanks to Alec and Valerie, I'll have to start again. Stay on the trail at all times…"

Everyone groaned as Reece droned on.

"She's a fucking bitch," Alec said out the side of his mouth as he glanced at the itinerary, his hair as glossy as tar in the sunshine.

"Should we just leave? I don't think I can take much more of her today." Valerie didn't want to admit defeat, but she really couldn't. What if Reece decided she was walking too slowly, or her knees weren't lifting high enough off the ground? What would she say then? What dark hollow would she force Valerie back to?

"No." The spark of his mischievous smile became a fire. "I say we put her in her place. She's been asking for it all weekend, but what she just said to you…she crossed the line."

Val considered the razor-sharp outrage in Alec's eyes. He seemed truly offended for her. She wanted to kiss him, hard. Instead she pressed her lips together.

"If she wants to act like we're still in high school," Alec continued, "we'll treat her that way."

Val's smile grew as large as a watermelon slice. "What are you thinking?"

"Well…" He stood back on his heels. "We have the empty side of this paper," he said, shaking the itinerary. "Maybe we hang a little something to Dora the Explorer's backpack."

"What, KICK ME?" she bantered. Her embarrassment melted away into camaraderie—the slow buzz that started in your stomach and traveled up and out when you were planning something you should not be planning with someone you couldn't wait to plan it with.

"That would be good." He considered. "I think everyone here would like to take a turn putting their foot up her bony ass, but she deserves something a lot worse. You got a pen?"

Val's pockets were empty but for her wallet and phone. She looked around and noticed a bag marked *Picnic Supplies* next to the trailhead. She rushed over and rummaged through. It was filled with paper plates, cups, and napkins but there were also markers, tape, scissors, and construction paper. *Is Reece planning to make us draw our own food?*

She pulled a red marker from the bag and put the tape in her pocket.

"Perfect," Alec replied, pulling the cap off with his teeth.

He flipped to the back of the itinerary and held it horizontally. He paused in thought for a moment before he wrote, *I'm only such a bitch b/c I need a good lay*, in large block letters along the center of the paper.

Val couldn't stop laughing. It was so juvenile, but it was also one of the most chivalrous things anyone had ever done for her.

"Masterpiece." He held it out and appraised his work.

"One more thing." Val reached for the paper. What Alec had was good, but she had a better idea. She remembered that Reece had printed her cell number across the top of the itinerary.

Val wielded the marker and beneath what Alec had written she added Reece's cell number and the words *Send Dick Pics*.

Alec's laugh was triumphant. "Damn Val, this hike just got a hell of a lot more interesting."

"For Reece especially," Val teased.

As they were preparing to leave, Cynthia hung the sign from Reece's backpack while she and Alec distracted her with fake apologies. It was almost too easy, Reece's ego lapping up every fake *I'm sorry* and *you were right* they fed her. For good measure, they continued far past when Cynthia gave the thumbs-up that the sign was in place.

Reece turned toward the trail. "Okay," she yelled over her shoulder. "Let's move out."

Cynthia had done great. The sign was affixed right to the top of Reece's backpack. The classmates on either sides of Alec and Valerie tittered as they took in the words and request. A few of them snapped photos of the sign.

Reece spun to face them. "What?"

"Sorry, I told a joke. It won't happen again," Alec said through laugh-clenched teeth.

"Whatever." Reece stepped onto the trail. "I said move out." She hiked like they were about to climb Everest.

"Guys," Alec whispered to their closest classmates, "you'd better do what she says." He pointed his thumb at the sign. "Also, those of you considering it, Instagram is great, but pass it along to everyone behind you via text first."

Laughter scattered through the group.

His boots pounded and her sneakers slapped the trail as they hurried to catch up to Reece. The anticipation was as strong as anything Val had ever experienced, buzzing and high in her throat. "This might be the best thing we've ever done together."

"It's pretty good," he said, moving his hand to the base of her spine, "but I'd pick a few other things for best." He squeezed his fingers into the soft flesh above her ass, giving her no doubt what *other things* he meant.

Wow, did she ever agree.

"Depending on how frisky the guys are feeling..." Alec pulled his hand away and put both out in front of him director-style. "It could actually be epic."

Val turned to check. Several of the guys from their class

were stepping to the side of the trail to shove their phones down their pants.

"It's about to get epic," she squealed.

He rubbed his hands together villainously. "I can't wait."

"Are you going to join in?"

"Only if you are." His brows flickered.

She stuck her tongue out in mock disgust. "No one needs a picture of that."

His gaze dripped down to her fly. "I'd frame a picture of that."

She followed his eyes. Her zipper was shiny gold in the sunlight peeking through the canopy of maples and elms above them. An alarm clock seemed to go off between her legs, buzzing away with no snooze button in sight. She considered finding a bush to shove him into to give him his own private showing when Reece's phone tinged.

Valerie could barely contain herself. Laughter started filling her like air, and if she couldn't let it out it might take her up into the sky like a balloon.

"This better be from Gideon or Georgia; they're almost as bad as you two," Reece said, glancing back at them. She continued to hike as she pulled out her phone. She clicked into it and gasped, dropping it on the trail floor and stopping everyone behind her.

"Everything okay?" Alec asked.

"Yeah." Reece's face was white. "Fine." She picked up her phone and stuffed it back in her pocket. "Let's keep moving—we have a lot of ground to cover before lunch." Her voice was shaky.

When the next text rang out, Reece ignored it. Alec turned to Valerie and lifted his eyebrow. Another text hit a minute later, but Reece kept trudging. She didn't even move to put it on vibrate. It had to be because she *would not*, *could not* act like anything was wrong. Their stupid perfect hike had to stay perfect, even though her phone was like a Chippendale's audition.

Soon the tings were coming as insistently as the birds chirping above them: another and another and another and another.

Val couldn't help but feel a sense of pride in her classmates. They were totally coming through—with dicks.

"Your cell phone is ruining my hiking experience," Alec said, flat faced, but Valerie could tell he was trying not to laugh. She could barely hold it in herself. She bit her lip so hard she tasted metal.

Reece's hands trembled as she took her phone from her pocket. She clicked into it with her eyes closed. When she opened them and glanced at her notifications, she let out a blood-curdling scream.

"We're definitely not going to see the wildlife promised if you keep making so much noise," Alec pressed.

Reece's face was as red as a tomato; her eyes watered in anger. She wheeled around and pointed at the space between them. "I don't know what's going on, but I know you're involved."

"What are you talking about?" Val managed, even though each word had a laugh around it.

The rest of her classmates gathered behind them, trying their best to keep their laughing in check, too. Cynthia was doing a terrible job, laughs escaping her lips like wheezes.

Reece's phone exploded with more texts, more of her classmates' dicks on her display. *Talk about a yearbook.*

"I see you!" Reece jabbed her finger into the crowd. "All of you. This is a federal offense."

"What are you talking about? What's on your phone, Reece?" Alec asked, finally gaining his composure.

"This," she hissed, spinning it, "all their penises." She flicked her chin at the crowd.

"But why would they be sending them to you?" Valerie asked.

Reece's mouth was open in an *O*. She was stumped. For all her planning this weekend she never could have expected this.

"Maybe there's a best dick contest or something. Is that on the itinerary?" Alec asked.

Her classmates' decorum shattered at that, laughter spilling around the group like a dam had broken. Comments shot at Reece from all directions.

"I'd win!"
"What about best balls?"
"Longest pubes, right here!"

Reece fixed her bloodshot eyes on Alec and Valerie. "You're ruining everything." Her phone exploded in even more texts.

"I'd say things are going perfectly," Alec replied, crossing his arms.

"My dick is too big for your phone."
"I'm the one who's not circumcised."

"Reece, they're just going to keep sending them until you text back," Alec urged, "so I'd go with the full beave if I were you."

Instead of responding, Reece ran back to the trailhead, the catcalls and guffaws of their classmates following her.

Alec put his arm around Valerie. It was the same half hug he offered her when one of her solos went well, or when she got into the all-state orchestra. He gave her a squeeze and pulled her in close. "Guess that means it's time for lunch."

• • •

Their classmates were still laughing and cajoling one another when they set up at the picnic area beside the lake. Reece had left in one of the rental vans, and for the first time that weekend it seemed like Alec's classmates were here for one another instead of whatever activity was listed next on the itinerary.

"I'm going to help pass out lunches," Val said, noting with her chin the cardboard boxes full of sandwiches. She was glowing, sparkling like the lake beyond the picnic tables. He'd helped to do that, and he wanted to do it a thousand times more.

"Don't you dare go Reece Freedland on me," Alec joked.

She placed a finger to her chin in mock thought. "Hmm, I am jealous about what she has on her phone…that alone might convert me."

Alec laughed. "I'd be happy to fill your phone up for you."

She eyed his belt buckle. "I do not have the data plan for what you're packing under there."

"We could test it out." His gaze went right to the button on her shorts. "Too bad you'll be busy waitressing."

"I just want to thank everyone," she explained.

"You're going to thank people for sending dick pics?"

Val's eyes danced. "You're damn right I am."

"In that case," he said and angled his body closer, "where's my thank-you?"

She met his stance and ran a finger along his bottom lip. "Later." Her fingertip lingered for just a moment before she headed off to take care of the sandwiches.

It was a good thing, because if she hadn't, he'd have pulled her back into the woods to get that thank-you now. He was continually thrilled by her wild streak. Especially because it was a side she seemed to reserve only for him. She'd always had a spark of rebellion, but it wasn't until this weekend that he'd realized how damn sexy it was.

Cynthia walked up behind him and slapped his back. "Nice work with Reece."

"That was mostly Val." A smile flashed onto his lips. *Send Dick Pics*? He let out a low whistle. She really was a dirty girl.

"She never would have done something like that on her own. She might have had the cherry-on-top idea, but that was you."

"Glad to be of service." He saluted.

He hadn't done it for any other reason than the way Reece had talked to Valerie. He could never stand up to her and the assholes in high school who'd made barking noises as Valerie took the stage or when she walked down the hall. He'd had his own jeers to deal with back then, but now, no one would ever get away with doing anything close to that ever again. Not that he could share that with Cynthia, or anyone really.

A best friend would do what he'd done, but what he'd felt when he saw Val's white face, the tremble of her lip, had nothing to do with friendship. It had to do with protecting his woman. *Mine*, a word he'd never thought he would use in any relationship—a word that made him dizzy with uncertainty filled his chest as he glanced over at Valerie again.

Would she be? Could she be?

Fuck, he had no right to be selfish. He had no right to fast forward ten years into three days. He wasn't even sure he wanted to.

"If nothing else, at least we can eat in peace," Cynthia concluded. "Reece would probably be telling us how to chew our food, so we made sure we didn't choke."

"Is that how the other meals have been going?"

Cynthia waggled her brows, two accusing caterpillars above her blue eyes. "I forgot you guys hadn't made it to a meal yet."

Alec was suddenly tongue-tied, not embarrassed certainly, but there was something that held him back from responding. The word *mine* was still banging around inside him unaccepted, unrequited.

"I hope you're making sure Valerie's getting all her vitamins and minerals," Cynthia continued with a wink.

Alec laughed. He didn't have to worry about Cynthia judging what was happening between him and Valerie; she just seemed happy it finally was.

He smiled easily. "It's my highest priority." He was glad to be joking around. Thinking seriously about Valerie was hard enough—talking about her, he couldn't even go there.

"You should probably think about some other priorities, too," Cynthia said.

"What, did Valerie say something to you?" A cold clutch of nervousness squeezed at his gut. It would take so little to knock over the bone-china-delicate relationship they had cobbled together this weekend. "I mean I know she told you about—"

"About your weekend arrangement," Cynthia interrupted. "Yeah, I'm fully up to speed. I guess I'm just wondering what happens after this weekend?"

It was a damn good question, one that, since that morning, he couldn't stop thinking about. Not at the top of his mind, but below everything like a lake all of his other thoughts floated on. He knew soon enough he would be drowning in it.

"That's not just up to me."

It was easier than answering her, because he had no answer—churning up that lake made him nauseous, dizzy, broke his skin into a cold sweat, the same symptoms as seasickness. He was a rock star who drank whiskey for breakfast—he didn't get "nauseous" about women, about a woman.

Cynthia squinted. Her bullshit meter was on high, as usual.

"She did say something," Alec exclaimed, faster than he'd intended, fast enough that he must have wanted to know the truth badly.

"About how she feels about you?" She smacked his back. "She doesn't have to," she added as she walked away.

Fuck, this was what he'd been pushing down since the second his lips touched Valerie's hand in that closet. The *what if* that had seemed to have become a part of his marrow—the answer that would change everything.

But he also understood to get those words from her, he'd need to offer up some of his own. Words he'd never planned on uttering in his life, let alone this weekend. But maybe he didn't have to use words.

"Alec."

He woke from his thoughts and found Val sitting under a tree with two lunch bags. The sight of her smiling in the sunshine, her hair shiny like melted chocolate, her skin glowing like she had a lantern in her belly, made all his uncertainty disappear and only one thought come into focus—*go to her, enjoy her while you still can.*

He headed over and lowered himself onto the grass. She handed him a Pepsi and popped hers open with a suggestive laugh. She took a long drink and punctuated it with an *ahhhh* like she was in a commercial.

"It really is so much better," she reasoned, taking out her sandwich.

He cracked open his own and took a drink. He'd honestly never thought about the difference between Coke and Pepsi. The other guys in the band had all kinds of riders on their contracts stipulating what was in their dressing rooms, but he never bothered. It seemed prissy to ask for something so specific, but prissy or not, he would always ask for Pepsi now.

The thought reminded him he'd be going back on the road in the winter. Even if he and Valerie were able to keep this going, he would have to leave her. Leave her to worry about a tour's worth of *what ifs*.

But she might leave him first and go to London—leave an

ocean of *what-if*s between them.

"You're sure you don't work for Pepsi?" he asked. "You aren't a part of some, like, new guerilla advertising campaign they're working on?" He unwrapped his sandwich and took a bite—turkey with mustard, his favorite.

Amusement flickered in Val's eyes, and she lowered her sandwich. He guessed it was peanut butter and jelly; she used to eat them like she was Popeye and they were her spinach. "Yes, women everywhere are luring men to vending machines for…" She trailed off.

"For what?" Alec insisted, staring at the inviting line between her lips before she pressed them together.

She stayed silent, her face glittering like the metal of their cans in the sunlight.

He smiled. "I guess my question doesn't make much sense considering I lured you."

She ripped at the crust of her sandwich as she considered what she was going to say next. "We lured each other."

Fuck, he wanted to touch her, kiss her. Just make out with her for hours under this tree, like they were back in high school. The grass mingling with her hair as his tongue mingled with her lips, kissing and kissing and kissing until their mouths and bodies ached.

He wondered if she was thinking the same thing.

"Regardless," he answered, managing to pull himself out of the fantasy, "I'm a Pepsi man now."

Saying that was easy. Saying he wanted to be her man was so much more complicated, something he wasn't even sure he could get to. Making her believe it after all the women he'd told her about for the last ten years might be impossible.

But did *he* believe it? That was the real question. Did he believe that she could finally count on him? That he could be the man she needed?

He swallowed. The word *no* bubbled up into his vision

like one of those Magic Eight Balls.

They sat in gluey silence, chewing on their sandwiches. If they'd been alone he would probably be nibbling on her ear, slicking his tongue down the center of her neck, teasing it between her cleavage. Their sandwiches would be thrown aside, their Pepsis upended and pooling on the grass as he went crazy on her.

Fuck, I need to stop. He glanced at her. Found big brown eyes that always knew exactly how to look at him, exactly what he needed at every moment. *How can I ever stop?*

"How'd the thank-yous go?" He couldn't care less, but he'd use anything to try and get devouring Valerie off his mind.

"They thanked *me*." She giggled. "It's too bad we're not still in high school; after this morning I could probably win class president."

Alec joined in her laughter while rolling the first part of her statement around in his thoughts. *It's too bad we're not still in high school.* Was it? Would being able to take back the invitation to New York change how unbalanced he felt about her now?

"What are you thinking about?" Valerie's eyes were enough to dismantle his insides.

About you, about us. "I'm still enjoying that look on Reece's face."

Val smiled, but it wasn't full or real. She knew he was lying, but was he if he wasn't sure how to tell her the truth?

Sex with Valerie was one thing, but fucking her over and over again didn't prove shit. He'd never seen what the kind of promise Valerie was waiting for looked like—real commitment. He only knew the kind of eternity where his parents lived.

He'd always blamed his father for the mess of his parents' relationship, but he saw now that it had been his mother and her choice to stay that was to blame for the mess of him. Her inability to protect him had forced him to protect himself however he could. With women that shield had been emotional. With Val that protection made him believe he could be the man she needed for this weekend only, but she was breaking through, crumbling his walls. All the protection in the world hadn't saved him from her kiss.

"I hope Reece skips the dinner tonight." Valerie's Pepsi-sweet exhalation filled the air. "The outfit I brought was not intended for ex-bully scrutiny."

"I'm sure you'll look beautiful," Alec replied, so quickly he almost tripped over his words.

Valerie's gaze stiffened. "Just promise you'll be there next to me in case there is a repeat of today."

He touched the top of her hand, tightened his fingers around it. He could do more than that. He had a stylist who could get designer clothes with a snap of his fingers, but he didn't want to get Val's hopes up until he had a chance to call and find out for sure. "Of course," he finally replied, filing the idea away. "Of course I'll be there next to you."

He might not be ready to promise her forever, but he could promise her that, at least.

Chapter Fourteen

Valerie lounged on the bed in their hotel room while Alec hung back in the Maserati and made some phone calls. She wondered if she should meet him at the door naked, or wait for him splayed out on the bed in her lingerie. There were three hours until dinner, more than enough time for him to get a real good look at what he'd said he wanted to frame and just enough time for her to give him the thank-you she'd promised.

But she also didn't want to seem too eager. Not that anything she'd done thus far had indicated she was anything but. She reined in her thoughts, clicked into her phone, and checked her emails. She wasn't expecting to find anything, which was, of course, why she did.

The London Philharmonic.

She said the words in her head at the same time she saw them sitting in her inbox. The email had been in there unread for hours. While Alec was cooking for her and ravaging her and making her wonder how she would ever be able to survive without his kiss, the answer she had been waiting more than a month for had arrived.

Her pulse beat into her neck, her palms itched, and her stomach flitted like a hummingbird's wings.

This was it. She clicked into the email. *We are happy to inform you… A week from today to accept… A chair in the woodwind section for the 2017-2018 season.*

The answer was yes. *Yes!* She let out a small squeal and bounced up and down on the bed. Happiness washed over her until another thought butted its way in.

What about Alec?

What about him? What was happening between them shouldn't change this, but she couldn't help wondering if it would. If they were dating, they would talk about how this would and could change their relationship. But because they were just friends who fucked, no matter how confusing her feelings were about it, they would not discuss what this meant for them.

How could she expect any different? They hadn't talked about how they felt, per her rule. The best they could muster was to talk about how much they liked fucking. Never once had they mentioned what it was doing to their minds and hearts.

Maybe their fucking was only doing something to her mind and heart.

She sat back against the headboard, glad she hadn't decided to go with the naked idea. She wondered what she would say. What he would say. She wondered if maybe this would finally shake loose the words that had been floating subconsciously in her mind. If the words she hoped Alec was also holding back would finally break free.

A few minutes later, Alec returned. He closed the door behind him and dropped his key on the dresser.

"What's up?" he asked.

"What do you mean?"

"Well, first of all you're staring at me, and second of all I know you. I know your expressions. The one on your face right now is *I have news, but I'm biting my lip to keep from spilling it.*"

"I'm not biting my lip."

His expression was insistent; his eyes were stained a darker brown. "Not now that you're talking, but you were."

Why was she stalling? She wasn't afraid to tell him, but she was afraid of what he would say back, or more specifically not say.

She took a deep breath. "I heard about London."

"And?" He stepped closer to the bed. He stood over her, blinking, his shoulders tensed, a breath lodged in his throat.

She could have just told him right away that she'd been accepted, but she wanted to see his expression. What would color his face when he knew the news was imminent? When she told him that she'd made it? What would his eyes do when she told him that she was leaving him, them? That she would not be visiting him in L.A. at all. That FaceTime would have to cut it.

"I got it," she said, trying to keep her face blank.

He paused, squared his body. It was imperceptible but as loud as a scream. His eyes shifted down, his lips pressed together. His expression said, *fuck, well I guess that settles it.*

Alec wouldn't want anything but for her to go to London. To follow and achieve every dream she ever had. But there was that pause. A pause that she wondered if before this weekend would have existed. A pause that could have a million meanings, but she was pretty sure this pause, on this day, in this room, with news that upended what could be something between them, was the pause of a decision being made for them.

He sat on the edge of the bed and pasted a smile on his face. "This is huge, Val. I'm so happy for you."

She nodded and tried to smile, too. It *was* huge, and she was happy. This was supposed to be everything she ever wanted in the world, but with a man sitting in front of her who she also wanted, the happiness was obscured by a smoky black film.

He grabbed her calf and squeezed. "You don't seem excited."

"I think I'm in shock," she said with a laugh.

His gaze deepened. "It's no shock that they took you. You're amazing. I've always known it, and now the world will."

Those words were the words of a friend, of a supporter. Where was his selfishness? Where was him asking when it was his turn, their turn?

But how could she expect that when she couldn't say it? When she couldn't admit that she wondered if she should go. That she would consider forgoing it for him, because even though he hadn't asked, this would mean she was saying no to him again.

He put his hands on his thighs. "What did your parents say?"

"I haven't told them yet."

"You need to." He rose and walked toward the door. "I'll give you some privacy so you can call them. We'll celebrate later," he added as he closed the door behind him.

She opened her mouth to tell him to wait, but it was no use. The conversation about London was over before it had even begun. Even if they weren't talking about it, she still couldn't help wondering what this would mean for them. Or did it change nothing?

She knew it was crazy, but she couldn't help wishing that he'd asked her not to go. Though Alec would never do that. Even if he loved her as more than a friend, even if he was starting to feel what she was starting to feel, the friend in him would always win out when her best interest was at stake.

But maybe *he* was her best interest. Maybe he should have been the life she had chosen all along.

There was a knock at the door.

Alec. He came back.

"You didn't have to knock," she said, pulling the door open.

A bellboy stood there holding a huge box with a ribbon around it, looking confused.

"Are you Valerie Barkin?"

She nodded.

"Delivery," he said, setting it in front of her and heading back down the hall quickly.

"I didn't order anything," she yelled to him, but he was already gone.

She stared at the box. What the hell was this? Had Reece sent her the school mascot's head or something? Or worse than that, was it a bomb?

She picked it up and tried to carry it into the room, but it was heavy. A lot heavier than she'd expected from the way the bellboy was carrying it. It was probably for the best, safer to open it in the hallway than the room anyway. She sat down in front of it and unwrapped it slowly, the ribbon soft and silky, the box smooth, gift-box cardboard. Not the way anyone would wrap a bomb or a severed head.

Inside she found a twenty-four pack of Pepsi, a slinky black dress, and a note.

Valerie,

Hopefully this will tide you over until dinner. I can't wait to see you there, in this.

Alec

Something was about to explode—her heart. It burst into tiny floating animated mini-hearts all over the inside of her chest. Tickling and teasing as they drifted like the inside of a snow globe.

Alec might not be able to talk to her about London, or about how he felt, but he sure knew how to show it.

Chapter Fifteen

Alec had performed in sold-out stadiums, on the Grammys, and even once for the president, but waiting for Valerie to open their hotel room door made it hard to breathe.

He'd meant what he'd said about London. He was happy for her, but he also couldn't help but wonder if fate was trying to make plans for him again. He shook his head and straightened his stance. Fate could go fuck itself. Tonight was all about him and Valerie and enjoying the time they had left together this weekend.

He'd gotten ready in Gideon's suite, so Valerie could put on the dress his stylist had sent without interruption. He wanted to pick her up for this night properly.

When she opened the door, the dress coiling over every curve like a second shiny skin and hitting right at the center of her creamy thighs, his chances at breathing became nonexistent.

Goodbye oxygen, hello Valerie.

"Hi." She finally spoke when he still couldn't. She glanced at him with a slight bite to her lip.

The dress shirt from the suit his stylist had sent to match Valerie's dress was so new it was making his neck and wrists itch, or maybe he would never get used to wearing fancy clothes. For Val, he thought he'd give it a shot.

For Val in that dress, he'd wear a suit every minute of his life.

"You look incredible," he finally said, letting out at least a little of the fever she'd awoken in him.

Her cheeks and neck bloomed, the dress even showing off pink petals of blush at her cleavage. Fuck, how was he going to make it through dinner?

"Oh good." She smiled, that smile like a sexy dress her lips wore. "I put on the right thing. I was not at all sure how to wear a twenty-four-pack of Pepsi."

Alec's limbs loosened from their stick-straight unease. "If anyone could figure it out, you could, but no, I meant the dress." He took the fabric at her shoulder in between his thumb and forefinger. "Incredible," he repeated. It was the only word that mattered.

He expected her to turn timid at all this attention, but instead she fingered the fabric of his collar mirroring him. "I never thought I would *want* you to have a shirt on, but this one is changing my mind."

"You like it?" he asked. "It's my symphony look. I even have a tie." He wrestled it from the pocket of his coat. "Unfortunately, I've never needed to learn how to tie one."

Before he could ask if she thought he needed to wear it, she subtracted the small space between them and kissed him, deep and long. His hands brushed the bare skin of her arms, the silken fabric at her back as he pressed into her. He pinned her body against the closed door of their room, his lips still plunging into hers, deeper, deeper, his fingers searching for more, wanting her in that dress jousting with wanting her out of it.

"Valerie..." He pulled back, intentionally leaving off the vixen nickname he'd given her, even though the implications of it were all he could see. "If we don't go to dinner soon, I'm going to end up throwing you inside that room and hanging this on our doorknob." He held up the tie.

"Who needs dinner?" she whispered. "I still need to thank you for the dress and for today."

Fuck, he was tempted. More than tempted, but sex could wait. If they only had one night left, he wanted to take her out on as real a date as he could muster. That was more important.

More important than your cock pounding into her with that dress pushed up around her waist? His abdomen wailed and his cock howled for her. But it fucking was.

"I want to take my time with you," he said, not giving away his real reasons for attending the dinner, along with sharing a blistering truth. "No interruptions and no itinerary crap hanging over us—just my lips and your soft, yearning skin and hours and hours to explore every bit of it."

She swallowed. Her eyes were immersed in fire like two comets. "I guess we should eat. Sounds like I'm going to be using up a lot of calories."

He reached for her hand, and they headed toward the elevators. He kept himself in the farthest corner, while she stood in the middle. The blistering heat inside that metal box was like a comet itself, set to shoot them into the depths of their desire if he even looked at her too long.

The doors thankfully opened onto the lobby.

"I hope we're not overdressed," Val said.

He'd managed to keep his hands off of her on the trip down, but it was a struggle, and with her words a new one emerged: Alec wanting to tell her *any time you wear clothes you are overdressed.*

The itinerary had said cocktail attire. Alec had no idea what that meant. To him cocktail attire was a flask.

"You look so amazing," he said instead, "people are going to want to go upstairs and change."

She gave his hand a squeeze. Her skin was radiant against black, but the color was only a part of the equation, the rest was all Valerie.

The ballroom was filling up when they arrived. Even without Reece's military precision pressing his classmates on, people had found places to sit and gotten drinks all on their own.

The tables were decorated with bouquets of flowers and candles. He glanced around for Gideon and when he couldn't find him, led Val to where Cynthia was already sitting along with Jacob Riedel and some of their band friends.

"I wondered if you guys were going to join us," Cynthia whispered to Alec as they hit the table.

"We almost didn't," he admitted, pulling out a chair for Valerie.

The thrum of desire hit him once again as he got a view of the back of Valerie in that dress—her milky shoulders, the wisps of hair at the nape of her neck, her ass. He fought against the erection threatening.

He could make it through dinner with all these people, but not with a boner.

The waiter came around and filled their empty glasses with water and white wine. Alec was never a wine guy, but he was going to stay away from the hard stuff tonight. Keep clear of what he usually used to numb. He wanted to be fully alert for Valerie.

"This is like the prom I never had," Valerie said.

"With alcohol," Cynthia observed, holding up her wineglass.

Valerie's remark brought Alec back to their prom night. She'd said she hadn't wanted to go anyway when no one asked her, and Alec didn't have the balls at the time to be the one to ask. The two of them spent prom night in Valerie's living room watching movies, nothing special, except for the fact he'd actually gone in the front door of her house. At least they'd been together. Her skin had been pale in the TV-made blue-white light, her eyes as dark as universes when she looked at him. She seemed to be waiting for something, maybe waiting for more.

Or had that been an illusion? When he'd tried to offer her more by asking her to go to New York, she'd said no. But was that because the *more* he'd tried to offer was too much? The more she might have wanted was just a kiss, a touch, a glance—a more that could have built into the more he had asked for if he'd just been patient.

"Wine isn't alcohol," Alec replied.

Jacob laughed. "But it does do in a pinch, doesn't it, dude?" He lifted his glass and clinked with Alec's.

Alec took a long drink. He supposed it did.

The waiters deposited plates in front of them. It had been a choice of steak, chicken, or pasta. Alec had ordered steak weeks ago. Val had ordered the pasta. She speared a piece and studied it closely before giving it a wary bite. Her eyes wandered to Alec's plate.

"You want some?" he asked, his mouth unintentionally full. He couldn't take Val looking at anything longingly and not being able to partake if he could help it.

That was never happening again.

"No, I don't eat steak," she replied firmly.

He swallowed what was in his mouth, took a palate-cleansing sip of wine. "You look like you want to eat steak."

Her eyes flickered. "I can never fool you, can I?"

He cut off a small slab and dropped it on her plate. "Why would you want to?"

She tried to work her butter knife into the steak.

"Besides, everyone knows not to order the pasta. It's

for vegetarians and I'm pretty sure most chefs make it with disdain."

"What are you, like, a cooking expert after this morning?" Having no luck with her butter knife, she lifted the steak to her mouth and bit at it.

"Were my eggs better than that pasta?"

Grease slicked Val's lips. "You know they were, Julia."

He leaned in to the sweet floral smell of Val. That juxtaposed against the animal hunger of her gnawing at steak made him hot for her all over again. He moved his lips to her ear. "Call me that all you want, I'll be her in the kitchen as long as I'm the name you're screaming out in the bedroom."

Her eyes widened then focused in desire. "How am I supposed to make it through dessert?"

"How about we screw dessert?"

She pressed her chest into his arm. "Or just screw."

• • •

Alec's eyes were all fire. He slipped a hand over hers. He looked so hot all cleaned up and classy. His brown hair was slicked back and his suit jacket made his chest even broader. The thought of unbuttoning his powder blue dress shirt, slowly exposing his bad boy tattoos underneath, forced her to squirm in her seat to soothe the ache.

How long would it take him to pull her the hell out of there? She was happy to be here with Cynthia and Jacob—*way to go, Cynthia!*—and Alec, of course. She loved being in the dress he bought for her, but she would much rather be out of it.

He started to help her to her feet when feedback filled the room. Reece was up on stage, tapping at a microphone in front of her. "Dinner is over, karaoke is next," she said, walking off the stage quickly.

Apparently Valerie and Alec hadn't totally ruined her. Though it was clear she was saying only what she needed to say. At least that meant Reece would stay the hell away from her. Though she was pretty sure she could take anything Reece flung at her in this dress.

"Karaoke," Cynthia said with a smile. "You have to sing, Alec."

He glanced at Valerie. "No one wants the rock star to upstage them."

"I do," Jacob said. "I'd bet everyone in here does."

Alec hesitated. "I think we are going to take off."

"No," Cynthia said, "sing at least one song. You can wait one song, right Val?"

She'd waited this long, she could make it through a song. Valerie put her hand on Alec's. "Go do what you do best."

He rose from the table and pressed his lips to her ear. "Ten minutes and we can go do the other thing I do best," he whispered, dropping a kiss on her cheek.

After all their hidden lust that weekend and their denied lust that evening, you'd think a swipe of his lips would feel like nothing, but that small, sweet gesture caused her heart to rise and throb—made her squirm in her seat again.

Cynthia met her eyes, raised an eyebrow.

Val shrugged, though it must have been clear there was a wash of pink all over her bare shoulders.

Alec joined a clump of their classmates who were already signing up for songs. Valerie didn't have to be in earshot to know they were all pushing him to go first. He whispered something to the DJ and headed up on stage. He situated himself in the center, hung his suit jacket on the microphone stand, and grabbed the mic.

"Hey everyone." His voice came through the speakers.

The room erupted in hoots and screams.

"I don't usually sing karaoke, but if I'm going to, I figured

I should sing a song I used to sing a long time ago. A song that means something to me, that means something to someone who means something to me."

Someone who means something to me?

Tiny bubbles formed and popped like champagne was poured all over Valerie's skin. She wasn't sure what song was going to come out of his mouth, but there was no doubt, it was for her.

She watched Alec on stage through blurry eyes, a thrumming heart. It only took her four notes to recognize the song. "Every Breath You Take." Alec's eyes fell on Valerie as words she couldn't believe she was hearing sprang from his mouth.

Oh can't you see, you belong to me. How my poor heart aches, with every step you take.

She'd heard him practice this song so many times when they were in high school. She'd given him pointers on tempo and the timbre of his voice, but this version was by far her favorite. For the first time ever he was singing this song to her. For the first time ever she heard those words in her heart.

The last lines burst out of him and he stepped back from the mic with a slight bow.

Valerie stood and clapped, trying to keep her welling eyes in check while the room around her erupted, too. Alec stepped off the stage and she ran to him.

They both stood for a moment in the roar of their classmate's applause as the next singer took the stage. She thought Alec might say something, but instead he watched her, waited for her.

She understood it was because it was her turn to admit what they both knew.

What was happening between them was real.

"Alec…" she finally said, but no other words would come. She was overwhelmed and of course while he'd sung those words, while she knew they were meant for her, he hadn't said them yet.

"Not as good as my guitar version, but I figured it would do." His eyes went soft. "Val, I…" he started, trailing off in the same way she had.

"I think it's time to get out of here," she said, leading him from the ballroom.

When they hit the hallway he stopped, his eyes intensifying to a blazing brown as he pulled her into an embrace so fierce it knocked the breath from her. She met his kiss, surpassed it—poured all her feelings into their gnawing, greedy lips. There were more things they would need to say to each other, but for now their kiss was enough.

A kiss she knew had nothing to do with rules, or expectation, or confusion, was everything in that moment.

They kissed furiously. Her hands played with the buttons on his shirt, his fingers trailed along her bare shoulders, and their bodies molded closer, closer. A molten heat rose that neither one could stop, until something struck Valerie, something familiar about this whole night.

"Hold on. You're *Pretty Woman*-ing me, aren't you?" She glanced up at him. "The expensive dress you bought me, the note, it's just like the movie," she insisted with barely a breath between her words.

Alec's face was suspiciously blank. "I don't know what you mean."

"And singing me a karaoke song was just like the piano scene!" Her voice rose in emphasis.

The small space between them was crackling with heat. "I don't need to follow a script to woo you, Valerie, but if you insist, what happens after the piano scene again?"

Oh, she knew exactly what happened and damn if she didn't wish she had a piano. But she did have an empty ballroom. She pushed open the door to the room closest to them. "I am not going to make it upstairs."

"I'm not going to make it five more seconds."

They stepped inside. It was an exact replica of the ballroom where the dinner was held with one important difference—it was completely bare.

"Let's finish the scene," he said, pulling her across the wooden dance floor toward the stage.

They climbed up onto it, and she pressed into him. "Is your concert over, or do I get an encore?"

He smoothed a finger along the skin of her arm. "My audience gets whatever she wants."

"Okay then," she said as she led him backstage.

It was set up the same as any she'd been in—a small corridor with wires and controls for the sound and lights. It felt the same, too, a place of endless anticipation, and she realized that was who she became when she was with Alec—anything could happen, anything *would* happen.

She hung her hands around his neck and he pinned her against the wall. He played with the zipper at the center of her back. "I want to take my time with you, Valerie, but my encore requires getting you out of that dress and once I do, nothing is going to stop me until I have you skin to skin screaming your throat raw."

She wanted that, oh wow, did she want that.

"We have plenty of time to take our time." She stepped back from him. "I think right now I'd like you to start your encore." Whether he knew it or not, she was still clapping for him between her thighs.

His eyes raked over her face. "I like the sound of that." He lowered her zipper. The dress fell at her feet. A strapless black lace bustier, matching lace panties, sheer thigh highs, and her heels were all that was left in its wake.

"And fuck," he breathed, "I really like the look of that. You are beautiful." He kissed along her neck. "Valerie."

While she loved the sound of her name on his lips, the way he said it like a song, she craved more.

"You're not calling me Dirty Girl." She wanted the words, the call, the primal need they engulfed her in.

"I thought I should call you Valerie now, since we're not just fucking," he explained.

Her finger played along the length of his jaw. "We may have taken the word *just* away, but we are most definitely fucking."

His hands fell to her hips and he grasped her, his hard, hot dick letting her know whether he called her it or not, she was his Dirty Girl.

She wanted to be both the woman he knew and the one he now craved. She took both sides of his shirt in her hands and ripped, several buttons popping off and falling to the floor like pieces of candy. "I didn't think you'd ever wear that again anyway."

A groan spilled from his lips almost as forcefully as his eyes swept over her, all over her. His chest heaved under his partially opened shirt, his tattoos screamed over his skin. His eyes were as dark as coal. "Dirty Girl, are you going to be able to handle the fuck that's coming to you after that?" He played with the delicate hairs at the nape of her neck as he cuffed his hand and pulled her mouth closer. His erection seared at her thigh.

She met his waiting embrace. "Only one way to find out."

His lips were a blush away from hers. "If you insist on that nickname," he said, "I'm going to make you earn it."

The heat in her cheeks traveled down to her abdomen and lower, flooding her, leaving her already wet panties sopping. "I haven't yet?"

He ran a finger down the side of the bodice, slowly tracing every curve. "We've barely gotten started." His hand advanced to her neck, over her collarbone, exploring the swell of her cleavage. "Turn around, put your hands against the wall, and spread your legs."

The sternness of his voice caused her lip to quiver, her stomach to twitch, but she didn't move.

His eyes bore into hers, as unrelenting as his expression. "At the beginning of this weekend I had to promise you an orgasm. I'm about to give you the most intense one of your life."

The possibility in those words was all the push she needed. She spun to face the wall and lay her hands against it. He forced a leg in between hers and pushed her ass up in the air. A finger met the zipper running down the spine of her bodice. He didn't unzip it, just scratched his nail along it. The sound, the touch making her legs tremble.

"Dirty Girl, you waiting for me like that, dressed like a pinup girl, has me so worked up I can barely stand it."

She made herself remember to breathe, her heart rate increasing because she couldn't see him. She could only feel him. His light-as-a-whisper fingers and his breath and his words, oh, those wicked words.

He pressed into her back, his erection scorching against the lace-covered cheeks of her ass. "Have you ever let someone take that sweet pussy from behind?"

She shook her head, not wanting to speak, afraid if she did her heart might fly out of her mouth.

He put a hand to the waistband of her panties and ripped them down before she could even get another breath out. "This is the kind of encore where I give you a standing *O*."

She heard a zipper unzip, a wrapper open, and he was inside her, pounding her slow and deep, his arms and hands on top of hers.

"Fuck, I didn't think it was possible, but you are even hotter from behind."

She strained down on him, the feel of him slapping

against her ass as he went deeper and deeper taking her over the edge. He kissed at her neck, licked at her shoulder, his breath in her ear coming as powerful as his thrusts.

He took one of her hands away from the wall. "I can touch you, but a dirty girl knows how to touch herself."

"Alec," she breathed, as he slid her hand lower, lower. He was taking her somewhere she'd never gone. Every time their bodies met this weekend she'd gone deeper and dirtier than she'd ever thought possible.

He found the spot he was looking for and guided her finger against it. The first contact with herself while he plunged inside almost made her legs give out. He pressed harder, leading her finger in a syrupy circle, and the second contact almost broke her in half.

He moved his finger away. "Just like that, Dirty Girl; you work that clit while I fuck you deep."

Hot, searing need trampled any embarrassment and she continued the teasing circles he'd started. Everything in that moment became her finger and his dick, working in tandem to bring her higher than she'd ever been. The first hint of release glided up from her toes still tight in her heels. The surge grew and rose from her ankles, sliding up her shins and thighs. Her legs shook as he continued to pound against her while her finger slicked a circle at her swollen core.

She slowed her movements; she was going to finish in seconds, and she wanted this to never end.

"Come, Dirty Girl," Alec said, "I'll be right here all night."

One hard swipe of her finger, one more enormous thrust and she did, convulsing around him. Her limbs went loose, but he held her up and kept pumping.

He kissed her neck, licked the back of her earlobe. "Get that finger working for round two. This time we're going to ride the wave together."

She was blind with relief, but the promise of more sweet

satisfaction, of being in that beautiful place at the same time Alec was, brought her finger down again.

"You feel so good," he said. "I could fuck you like this forever."

Valerie focused on the word—forever—let it slip in and spin around in her mind.

"Forever," she repeated, the word taking root. They had been best friends forever and now they could, they would, be more.

Alec's thrusts turned feral, primal, and the speed of her finger met them. She was on the heels of another orgasm. It was speeding at her, a crash she couldn't avoid. The word he'd used was the word she thought of—*forever, forever, forever*—just as the hot release hit. Her thighs tensed as he jerked against her, a choked groan escaping as he pounded her with one last thrust.

He was still inside her, gasping hot against her shoulder, laying small kisses there as she worked to catch her breath. He eased out. She heard the sound of the condom being tossed, his boxers being pulled back up.

He guided her panties back on. "If I stare at your naked ass for one more minute we are never getting out of here." He laughed, giving it a squeeze.

She turned to face him. "Why do we have to leave?"

"We don't, but we do have a room to ourselves upstairs, just an elevator ride away." He slanted his mouth over hers, his lips whisper light. "I want to spend the rest of the night kissing you."

It was sweeter than he usually was, but she certainly wasn't against it.

"Just kissing?" she joked.

His eyes turned dark with significance. "We have years and years to make up for, Valerie, and it starts with every missed kiss."

Chapter Sixteen

Valerie snuggled over to Alec's side of the bed. It was warm but empty, sunlight floating over his pillow. The shower was running. She was hoping to be awoken by a kiss, since that was how she'd been put to sleep, but the smell of him and the whisper of warmth he'd left behind would have to do for now.

She inhaled against his pillow. Losing herself in his scent—leather and sex—she allowed it to pull her back to the two of them in bed last night. After they got back to the room they spent the night making out as he'd promised, just kissing for hours and hours.

She hugged herself and replayed getting lost in his lips again and again as he counted each kiss, whispering numbers into her mouth. He was well into the hundreds before they fell asleep.

She couldn't leave him and go to London now. At the very least she needed to tell him she didn't want to, that she would consider declining her seat with The Philharmonic to see what they could turn into. She still had her spot in Philadelphia. She could apply for London again next year, or maybe even for the L.A. Philharmonic.

It was crazy and reckless, but it also seemed like it might be the best decision she'd ever made. How life was with Alec. How she wanted her life to be now—like she was falling, but he was there to catch her.

She picked up her cell and read through the email from The London Philharmonic again. Her dreams were right there on the screen, but they were also behind the bathroom door. Over the course of the weekend Alec had become the man she'd been waiting for. He'd shown that he wanted to be that man.

Ten years ago he'd asked her to take a chance on him. Saying no to London would show she was truly ready, would be the ultimate way to say yes.

Alec stepped out of the shower with a towel wrapped around his waist. His taut chest and block-like abs were on display, tattoos shiny with water droplets.

"What is it?" he asked, the steam from the bathroom flowing all around him.

"What do you mean?" The air in front of Val's eyes went blurry, her heart roared like a thousand oceans in her ears. Why was she so nervous? She just needed to tell him and then everything would be okay. He would catch her.

"Valerie." A smile played on his lips. "Don't act like I can't tell when something is on your mind."

She could never hide anything from him. She never wanted to again.

She slapped his side of the bed, calling him to her. She was ready to say it all, but she needed him close—needed his arms within reach, his lips within reach.

He sat down on the bed beside her, making the sheets damp.

"I want to talk about London," she finally said.

He nodded, but his face was pinched. "Okay."

"I'm thinking what we have now is too new for me to be in another country for a whole year. I'm thinking about turning it down." The words exited her body and instead of being caught by him, seemed to float between them like dust. She wrung her hands, the soft scratch of her fingers the only sound in the room.

"Are you nuts?" he finally replied, his voice sharp, droplets of water from his hair dribbling on his bare shoulders.

She'd been prepared to hear *we can make it through anything*. Or, *I was wishing you would tell me that, but not even an ocean can keep us apart*. Instead his tone was firm.

He rose from the bed. "It's too big of an opportunity. You're going."

She managed to suck in a breath, but it stung. "I think that's my choice."

"Then why the hell would you be stupid enough to turn it down?"

"Us," she said, the word hitching in her throat.

His glanced skittered; he looked down, his eyes anywhere but on Valerie. "This weekend has been great, amazing even, but I…" He moved his hand between the two of them. "*I am not what you change your life over*."

She heard the words under that. *You are not what I change my life over. We are not what you think we are.*

She hated how beautiful he looked in the sunlight with the fog of the shower behind him, his face freshly shaved, his hair a jumble of wet wisps along his brow. She hated that she still wanted to kiss him. She hated that their next words would determine if she ever would again.

"But last night…" She fought her watery eyes, stupidity raining down on her. She was falling, falling, and he was walking away. Her heart slackened, as if someone had thrown it bloody and beating against the wall, and now it was slithering to the floor to take its last gasping beat.

She was an idiot. Alec hadn't promised her anything. She had turned what he'd done, what he'd said, into a promise of forever. He'd never given her that.

He'd said the word. But he'd never used it the way she'd taken it. He'd said he wanted to fuck her forever, and that didn't mean anything.

He looked away, not even correcting what he had to know she was thinking. "What if something happens two weeks from now, or a month from now? You'll regret you didn't go—"

"Something?" she interrupted. "Or you mean someone."

Her nagging insecurity rose as she fell even further. When he had his choice of everyone in the world, why would he choose Valerie?

He rocked on his heels. "So that's why you want to stay, you don't trust me?"

She'd thought it was because of them, because of what they could be, but she knew his question was as true as anything. As true as the lie she'd been telling herself all weekend. *I am good enough for Alec. He is ready to be solid for me.*

"What does it matter when you don't want me to stay anyway?" Her words flew faster.

"So you *don't* trust me," he repeated.

She looked down, swallowed acid.

He shook his head slowly. "What have I ever done to you to make you not trust me?"

"Why are you changing the subject?"

"Why are you avoiding the subject?" His question wasn't thrown back in anger, but laid at his feet like a bridge.

Even so, she still couldn't respond. She wanted to trust him. She wanted to trust that what they had could last on two separate continents, in two separate time zones, but that didn't mean she believed it would.

He sighed. "There are all kinds of things that can go

wrong, Valerie, that have nothing to do with someone else."

"It's good to know you've been cataloging them." It came out nastier than she'd intended, but she needed to replace the air in her veins with fire. Her pain with anger, or there would be nothing left.

• • •

He sensed a pulsing in his jaw. "That's not what I meant."

"It's hard to know. I'm starting to wonder if anything you say is the truth." She pressed her lips together.

How had this gone south so quickly? This was why he'd never gotten in too deep. He was terrible at digging his way out. "I've never lied to you."

"You're right," she replied, "I've been the one lying to myself, believing you could actually care."

His stomach became a rock, a weight that seemed to be towing him down into an abyss. At times like this he would look for Valerie to save him. For once, he would be the one to save her. To make sure she didn't throw an opportunity like this away carelessly.

"How can you say that? I'm telling you to go to London because I care." His shoulders fell, and he tightened his towel. "I don't understand why you're upset." He'd said what he'd said for Valerie's own good, because he wanted what was best for her.

Unfortunately, he was not what was best for her. In a choice between him and London, London had to prevail. He wished he could be exactly who she needed, the man who could offer her the forever she dreamed of, but because he couldn't, he would not stand in her way. He would do for her what she'd done for him ten years ago when he asked her to move to New York—be the voice of reason. No matter how far down into the abyss life without Valerie took him, he would not allow her to follow him down.

"I'm not angry you're telling me to go." Her eyes were burning, the usual brown obscured by black smoke. "I'm not even angry at all, I'm hurt. Hurt you wouldn't even talk through me wanting to stay for one second."

"I can't be the reason you stay." His lips burned from his words, but couldn't she understand that throwing her life away on him was a terrible bet?

"Why?" she asked, her face pink with insistence.

His chest constricted, making each breath feel like it was his last. Hell, it might as well have been. He couldn't make the promise she needed to hear, and he couldn't tell her the truth. She wanted a husband, a partner, and he was neither of those things. "You know why."

"You're trying to punish me for saying no to you ten years ago. You're trying to show me how it feels." Her words came out fast, careening from her lips.

"No," he said, fighting to keep his composure. "I just know you made the right decision then, and I'm not going to let you make the wrong decision now."

"So you're telling me not to choose you. That's what you're really saying."

"Even without London, but especially because of it." His throat thickened. "I'm not the guy you should choose. We both know I'm not the guy you can count on. I'd like to be, but I wasn't ten years ago, and I'm not now."

"What? I'm supposed to just go back to normal now? Oh right, of course. Our weekend is over. My expiration date is past due. You can find someone else to fuck," she spoke quickly.

His insides seemed gray. "How can you say that?"

"Because you can't say anything that I need you to say, you can't do anything I need you to do."

"Valerie." He opened his arms. "I'm still right here."

She stayed on the bed, wringing her hands.

Why wouldn't she come to him? "Valerie," he tried again, his arms still out.

She kept his gaze but didn't move to embrace him.

How could he expect her to, when she couldn't be at all sure how long he'd continue to hold on? He couldn't see a time where he would let go, but that wasn't the same thing as forever.

"I'm through with being your backup," she finally said, "being the one you call when everyone is busy, who you text when everyone else is asleep."

He let his arms fall to his sides. His body was hollowed from her words and from his realization that maybe he didn't have the capacity to make this okay anymore. "That's how you view the last ten years? You mean something to me. I don't know how you can't see that." His eyes stung. "How is it wrong for me to want you to live your life?" The question hung there like a rope, but she wouldn't grab onto it.

"What's wrong is you don't feel like fighting to stay in it. But why should I be surprised? You are your mother's son." Her eyes widened, as if she was surprised by how cruel her words had been. "Alec…" She rose as if to apologize.

He reeled back from her and held his hand in front of him. The truth was out. That was what she really thought and why she didn't trust him—she thought he was weak. He'd believed his body was empty, but he realized now it was actually full to drowning. His blood had become water, and with that sentence it had turned to ice.

"I've never gotten to experience your bad side, Valerie. I have to say it's ugly."

Her eyes were dark and shiny as she exhaled. "Well, I've never been on your fuck-them-and-leave-them side and I have to say, it's cliché as hell."

They stared at each other for seconds that became

interminable minutes. Neither one of them spoke. There was only the silence that said it all.

He put his hand to the side of his face, kneaded at his temple, the pain starting to throb. He couldn't do this anymore. He shook his head, trying to wrench the ache free, and walked back toward the bathroom. "Good luck in London."

He waited behind the closed door, listening; his breath like the insistent pulse of a countdown clock. He thought she might knock, might whisper through the wood that their fight had gone too far, but instead the door of their hotel room slammed, echoed, and the room collapsed into silence.

Chapter Seventeen

Fuck. As quickly as Valerie had walked into his life she was running the hell out of it thanks to his baggage. But it wasn't like she was innocent, either. He might have been willing to try at a relationship if she went to London, but she didn't trust him enough to even consider going.

Didn't believe he could stay true to her after being her best friend for fourteen years. But she wasn't only asking him to stay true. She was asking him to be the one. The one she had been waiting for.

While he wished he could be that man, wished he could say, *yes I will be your life now*, he could not. It had hurt when she hurled it at him, but he *was* his mother's son—someone who did not fight, who did not leap. Who let the world make his decisions for him.

He stepped out of the bathroom and sat on the bed, Valerie's perfume assaulting him, punching his already ravaged gut.

Fuck this place.

He scrolled through his phone to call for his plane and

felt a stab when he saw Valerie's text stream.

He couldn't call her to make him feel better this time—maybe ever again.

He clicked on Gideon's number, but it went to voicemail. He swallowed a shudder. He couldn't remember the last time one of his calls went to Val's voicemail. The last time she didn't respond to one of his texts.

He'd lost that now, too.

His finger hovered over the number for his plane. He knew he should want to be alone. He should be mountain angry and kicking and pounding and hating, but in that moment his heart screamed for someone to talk to.

He dropped his phone on the nightstand. He didn't want his plane. He didn't want to run. He wanted someone to listen, someone to hear him. He breathed in again, each petal of her perfume stabbing him like tiny knives.

She was gone, because she couldn't trust him and because he couldn't trust himself. The echo of her rang through the room, mirroring the emptiness she'd left in her wake. Without her, who did he have?

He got dressed quickly and headed downstairs, hoping he might catch Gideon at breakfast. He scanned the ballroom, but he wasn't there. All his classmates seemed tired, hungover, and ready for this weekend to be done.

He knew exactly how they felt.

He spied Randy up at the omelet bar. "Have you seen Gideon?"

"I think he's out by the pool," he replied. "He and Georgia got into a whole thing earlier." He shook his head. "Looks like everyone's pussy machine is coming up empty."

Alec fought the urge to shove Randy's face into a hot pan. "You're really a dick, you know that?"

"That's what my wife tells me." He smiled, remorseless.

Alec recognized that look. It was the same one he

displayed before this weekend. The same armor he wore with women. Why the hell had he let Valerie shed him of it? He was nothing but raw nerves underneath. Nothing but everything he never wanted to feel. His head began to pound again, a headache gripping tight to his temples and squeezing. He clutched the back of his neck, hoping to knead it away, but it only intensified. *I am my mother's son and my father's prisoner. Even now he's here reminding me I'll never be good enough for Valerie.*

He headed out to the pool and found Gideon sitting up on a chaise talking to Brandon White.

Fuck, this fucking morning could suck his fucking dick.

Alec didn't want to deal with Brandon ever, but definitely not right now. Maybe Gideon had the right idea hanging with him, though. Being with the people everyone had always told you that you were meant to be with hurt too much.

Why didn't Gideon call me to talk about Georgia?

His jealousy was silly, but understandable after what had happened with Valerie. As was the thought he couldn't let go of. Maybe no one would ever need him again.

He headed out the side gate of the pool and around the parking lot to the Maserati. He sat in the driver's seat and stared at his phone.

No Val, no Gideon, no one. Without even thinking, he clicked into the phone and called his mom. She answered on the first ring.

"Alec, I don't want to talk about the house anymore."

He bit his lip. The only people he cared about in this world were his mother and Valerie, and he couldn't make either of them happy. His mother because she'd never believed she deserved to be, and Valerie because he didn't believe he did, either. If only he could have stopped her. Pulled Valerie to him and held her until all their terrible words were used up, until just the two of them remained. But her words had hurt him, too, hurt him enough to keep him from reaching out. Hurt him because he understood exactly why she'd said them.

"I'm not calling about that," he replied, but why had he called? What guidance could his mother give him about relationships?

None, other than to take shit because it's all you're worthy of.

"Oh," she responded, her voice more chipper. "Did you tell Valerie I said hi?"

"Yes, Mom, several times," he mumbled.

He wanted to say more. Tell his mom what had happened. Tell her everything he couldn't tell Valerie, everything he should have told Valerie.

Ask if it was enough.

But the words stayed churning inside him. If he said them, admitted them, he was done for. He sat back in the seat and caught another whiff of Valerie's perfume. The scent took over all his air. He was drowning in the hole she'd left, the hole he'd forced her to leave. Bigger than just this weekend, bigger and emptier than anything he'd ever known.

"What did she say?" his mom asked.

He'd forgotten his mother was on the phone. "She said hi, too."

Memories flooded him. Val's shocked laughter at each oddly timed mention of his mom's greeting. The way she squealed when he first touched her, the way she moaned when he last did. The way their final kiss had been interrupted by sleep, and how that turned it into something that they still hadn't finished.

That they might never finish.

"Such a sweet girl. Did you guys have a nice weekend together?"

Together—they weren't that anymore. In fact they'd never been further apart. The distance of London was nothing compared with what the discussion of it had wrought. How could he have let her leave their hotel room? Pushed her further away than a continent, hurled her into the black with him by trying to shield her from it.

"Yes, Mom." His eyes started to water before he could stop them. He wondered if he'd ever find anything close to what he'd had that weekend again—with Valerie, ever again.

Was this it? Fourteen years of friendship and who knew how many years of what could have been more, over, just because they were both too scared to trust. Too stubborn to be the one to say, *let's believe.*

"I'm so glad. She always knew how to make you smile."

He swallowed. She had, ten years ago, ten hours ago, and even before ten minutes ago. But now there was only stiffness in his chest, a heaviness overtaking him that made him want to forget, made him want to pick up the Maserati and hurl it at the sun.

It was a pain he didn't know he was capable of feeling, pain that terrified him—pain that his father's blows had taught him to suppress, to only feel physically. He pressed his hand to his forehead, waiting for the familiar headache to grip and grab, but tightness in his lungs, a twinge in his heart were all that assaulted him. Valerie might be gone, but he'd carry her there.

"I know I wasn't always what you needed," his mother said, "I know I'm still not, but I'm glad Val is. I'm glad she can be."

His heart churned, bloodless. A chill rocked him so strongly it seemed to be shaking him by the shoulders. But he was enduring. He was still here—barely, but he was. He never wanted to feel this again, but he also knew that if he had to, he could bear it. It was worth bearing for the pleasure on the other side of the knife of love.

Love. The word came again softer.

That was what he should have told Valerie. *I want you to go to London because I love you. I want you to want to go because you love me.*

Alec couldn't speak. Was it too late? Was it enough now to tell Valerie he loved her, to ask if she would love him even with everything he carried?

"Alec, are you there?"

"Yes, I'm here." He was, and he would be for a lot more years, years he didn't want to spend wondering, or missing, or hurting.

Years he didn't want to waste anymore.

He might not be the man Valerie should count on, but he could be the man she would count on.

"Mom, I'm selling the house. I can't keep trying to rescue you." His words came quickly, and with them something lifted and was released.

She breathed out. "I'm not your burden anymore, Alec."

Maybe he didn't have to be his own burden anymore, either. He'd carried that scared little boy as armor because he'd been too afraid to let him go. Too afraid to be the kind of man he deserved to be. The kind of man Valerie deserved.

He didn't want to be his mother's son or his father's prisoner anymore. He wanted to only be Valerie's.

Chapter Eighteen

Valerie pounded on Cynthia's door. Tears streamed down her face and dripped onto her neck, leaked into the cleavage of her tank top. She'd been so upset she left the room in her pajamas. She didn't even have her phone or her wallet.

What if Cynthia isn't here? Damn her heart for making her brain stop working.

That had been the theme of this whole weekend. Alec making her stupid body ignore her good sense. She saw Alec's eyes, his sad, disappointed eyes when he claimed she didn't trust him. Her stomach listed.

She could blame him all she wanted, but it didn't change that she hadn't been willing to believe that he could stay faithful to her when she was a continent away.

But it wasn't just London. If they were both in L.A. there would be times they would be separated for hours, or days, or weeks, or even sadly, minutes, and her concern would be the same regardless of the distance or time.

She would always wonder—*am I enough for him?*

Trust was an easy way to explain a hard truth. How could

she trust him, when she didn't believe she was the kind of woman he should want?

She gulped, tasting salt. She couldn't keep being disappointed, couldn't keep expecting more from him or from herself.

She knocked again, stuck her ear to the door. Cynthia had to be there. Valerie couldn't go back to her room, couldn't delve back into the broken shards of their relationship that she'd left there.

She fisted her hands to pound again. A throb ran through her, hot and hard. She hadn't left any hurt behind in that room. She was still carrying it all.

Cynthia finally pulled open the door. Her hair was wet and she was in a robe. "Meth Cupid paid me a visit. You just missed Jacob," she chirped.

"Congratulations," Valerie managed, trying to paste a smile over her tears.

Cynthia noticed Val's wet face and her own crumpled. "What happened?"

"Alec." Just saying his name squeezed at her chest.

Cynthia looked up and down the hallway. "Where is he? I'm going to kill him."

"He's still in our room. Can I come in before the gossip mill has even more fodder from us this weekend?"

"Of course." Cynthia moved to the side and closed the door behind them.

Her bed was unmade and rumpled, the rumple that Valerie recognized as having had an amazing night last night. The same way her bed had looked before she'd brought up London. Before Alec forced her to see that she was no more ready for a relationship than he was. Valerie wished she could rewind, enjoy the moment before he stepped out of the shower for a little longer. When the only thing in the world was basking in the sanctuary they had made of their bed.

"I'm sorry," Valerie said, standing uncertainly in the middle of the room. "You don't want to deal with this right now."

Cynthia glanced past her, her cheeks blazed, and she ran to pull up the comforter. "No, it's fine. I'm not supposed to see Jacob until after breakfast. I have plenty of time." Cynthia sat down on the bed and gestured for Valerie to join her. "Come talk to me."

Valerie paused.

"Don't worry, we weren't on top of the comforter."

Valerie let out a soggy chuckle. "I wasn't even thinking about that."

"Well, we weren't in case you're wondering. It's clean. Or you know, relatively clean."

"I'm happy for you, Cynthia," Valerie said, forgetting her morning for a moment.

"I know." Cynthia smiled so wide it could have filled its own bed. "But really Valerie, you're crying, or at least you were. That trumps gushing about Jacob."

Valerie nodded.

"So," Cynthia said, pressing with one word in the way only someone who has known you for years can.

The words that had been churning inside burst out. "I was stupid to start anything with Alec. He might care about me as a friend, but he's not capable of more."

She didn't add that even if he would have agreed she shouldn't go to London, they would have had this same fight a week from now, or a month from now. While she had been blinded by his attention, she hadn't been blinded enough to be able to see she deserved it. Her mouth went sticky and bitter. She wondered if she'd ever believed it. If even ten years ago when Alec had asked her to move to New York the reason she'd said no had less to do with him, and more to do with not trusting he could stay interested in someone like her.

Not when he had the world ahead of him.

"He sure seemed into you," Cynthia soothed.

"Into fucking me. Into being my friend," Valerie replied, playing with the bottom of her shorts. "Not into the place beyond both those things." Her words felt empty. It was what she thought, not what he'd actually said.

Not what she'd felt when he looked at her, when he kissed her.

"What happened? Did he break up with you?"

It stung to breathe. "We were never together, so no."

But that wasn't what had bothered her. She and Alec didn't need labels like that. What broke her was that when the angry words were through, only silence answered. She exhaled and stared at her hands. She couldn't even tell *Cynthia* what she was feeling; no wonder Alec had turned his back on her. She'd thought he couldn't talk to her about London because he was closed off, but really they both were. It was why they'd gravitated to each other years ago. It was why even now they sat in separate rooms wondering if they were going to live separate lives but not doing anything about it.

Cynthia watched her, waited. She wanted the real story.

"I found out yesterday I was granted a seat in The London Philharmonic for next year." Valerie wiped her nose. "I told Alec this morning I was thinking of not going, because of us."

"Oh," Cynthia said, her face a wash of understanding. "I guess he didn't agree."

"He told me I was nuts. He told me he wasn't the guy I should change my life over. He wasn't the guy I could count on." She piled on all Alec had done, but she still couldn't bear to tell Cynthia why she'd actually considered not going to London.

"The Alec I know would never let you turn that down." Cynthia glanced at her tentatively. "Not the guy he was ten years ago and not the guy he seems to be now."

"But if what he feels for me is real, shouldn't he want to always be with me?"

Cynthia pursed her lips. "He might not always have the best way to say things, but I think that's why he's telling you to go. If he didn't care he would let you make stupid decisions like turning down the Philharmonic, which, no offense, Valerie, was a monumentally asinine idea."

Valerie sighed. "But we'll never last that far away from each other."

"Did you ask him if he wanted to try?"

She hadn't, but how could she? Actually say the words *do you want to be with me?* What if he said no?

Alec might have wanted her to go to London because he cared about her, but did that matter if she hadn't believed it?

But, why shouldn't she? Every kiss and touch from Alec was proof she'd left *Barking* far behind. Every time she allowed him to adore the woman she was now, the echoes of her past disappeared. She wasn't that girl anymore. She was a woman who Alec wanted, a woman who wanted him. Each time their bodies met had been a letting go, an acceptance that she deserved his attention, that she deserved him.

"No, I didn't," Valerie admitted, "but I think it's more complicated than that."

"What relationship isn't? You guys have been friends for so long, you probably don't even know that it's okay to fight, to hurt, to lose, to compromise."

"We do so," Valerie countered.

"You might know that separately, but I'm guessing you don't know that together."

The words hit Valerie like a brick to her stomach. Maybe they didn't. They never had to work at their friendship, it just was—easy, comfortable, casual Al and Val. When it got too hard they both got scared. They both didn't know how to deal with it. They both reinforced the walls that had kept them apart since Alec had asked her to move to New York. Had kept either one of them from asking, *What are we? What can we be?*

Maybe the answer of silence wasn't the last gasp of their relationship. It was the first breath of something that wanted to begin if just one of them was strong enough to ask. To say what they really wanted without fear.

Cynthia touched her knee. "So what are you going to do? You're not going to leave things like this, are you?"

"I don't know if I have a choice. I said some things I can't unsay.

Cynthia sat back, her blue eyes clear. "Words said in anger don't mean anything, Valerie, they are a shield."

"But we both said them. We both held shields." *Mine had spikes on it*, Valerie thought, recalling the line and curve of each cruel letter she'd uttered. *You are your mother's son.* How could she have said that to Alec? To the one person in the world who had never been callous to her.

"Maybe you guys aren't ready to put them down yet." Cynthia shrugged. "Two people can be absolutely perfect for each other, but that doesn't mean anything if they aren't willing to risk giving it a try."

"We hurt each other." Valerie's stomach became a tight fist punching her ribcage. "Alec and me."

Cynthia's eyes clung to hers. "But you found each other, too."

Valerie's eyes stung. They had and now they'd lost each other. She started to cry again, so hard she thought the tears might leave scars on her face.

"Listen, don't make any decisions now. You're upset. He's upset. Take a shower. Go back to your room and get some clothes and we can have some breakfast."

"I'm not hungry." Valerie pouted, thinking of breakfast with Alec from the day before, wishing she could be back there. Wishing the two of them could have stayed in that house away from all the noise of the real world forever.

Forever. The word hit her again. It was what she thought she wanted with Charles, but she realized now losing him didn't come close to this. Losing Charles was like losing a game of chess. Losing Alec was so much larger, because she hadn't been playing to win. That was where real loss came from. It hit you without warning because you weren't even part of the game.

"At least take a shower," Cynthia pressed. "You can borrow some of my clothes."

Valerie nodded. She could do that, but beyond the shower and getting dressed she wasn't sure. Would she see Alec back in the room when she went to retrieve her phone and wallet? Or would he take his private jet out of Kenmore and out of her life?

No, she didn't want a repeat of ten years ago, of a life without Alec.

She would find the strength to be the one to ask the question this time. New York or London, the idea was still the same. It was her turn to ask if Alec wanted to leap.

Chapter Nineteen

A few hours later, Valerie walked down the hall toward her room holding one of the bouquets on the tables from last night. She felt silly, but they were the only flowers she could find on such short notice. Men who screwed up made things better with flowers, and since she didn't know what else to do, she'd figured why the hell not.

Alec had not checked out yet—she'd been able to find that information easily enough. She hoped beyond hope that he was still in the room. That he wouldn't be able to leave things between them this way, either.

Her heart plucked at quadruple tempo in her chest. She didn't know what Alec would say, but her words were clear. *I want this. I want you.*

She squeezed the stems tighter in her hand, took a deep breath, and walked the rest of the length to her room. Cynthia had gotten her an extra key from the front desk. She stuck it in the lock and took a deep breath before opening the door.

She stepped inside ready to shove the flowers in his face and tell him everything, but the fear she'd had on entering the room and having Alec reject her had been replaced with an icy punch to the solar plexus. Her luggage was still there, but Alec and his belongings had been cleared out. There was just a quiet, empty room that still smelled of him, still held all the notes he played, all the words he'd said, all the kisses they'd shared, all the almost they could have been.

But he was gone.

He'd left without even trying. He'd left before she could even try.

She couldn't move. Her body was as heavy as a boulder with the realization that Alec was out of her life, maybe forever.

Tears started to fall when her phone dinged from the nightstand. She picked it up and found a text from Alec.

You busy?

Her heart started to pound even harder, the tears in her eyes wondering if they should be happy, sad, or angry. Was this a peace offering, or was this him trying to see if they could just be friends again? If things could go back to the way they used to be?

The thought made her ill.

Yes, very, she texted back, afraid to respond with anything that would indicate anything. She was ready for a truce, but not of the friendship variety.

That's too bad. There's something down in the lobby I think you're going to want to see.

What did that mean? She didn't like how elusive he was being. She had come to find him prepared for a whole lot of truth. Her hand hovered over the letters on her phone and she considered her response when another text from him flashed onto the screen.

I'll be here waiting. I can wait forever for you, Valerie.

Forever.

And I will, his text continued.

Her hands trembled, making the words blurry, but the word she needed was there—*forever.*

Those seven letters sent her running down the hallway to the elevator, her heart in her throat and her tears drying in the rush of the wind. When it didn't come after maniacally pushing the button, that word sent her down the emergency stairs two at a time. She was out of breath when she opened the door to the lobby.

She thought Alec would be standing there waiting for her, but she didn't see him at first glance. He probably assumed she'd taken one of the elevators, so she looked along the line of them, across each of the couches, up at the front desk, at the concierge, but he was nowhere to be found.

Her phone dinged.

Gift shop, a text directed.

She rushed over to the gift shop, her heart careening around her chest like a rocket, her skin a sparkle of nerves, but Alec still wasn't there. Instead, she found a guy manning the cash register, rows of candy, and souvenirs. She scanned the walls, hoping to find a clue, and paused at the magazine rack. Alec's *Rolling Stone* magazines were still hanging in a line, but there was something different about them.

She stepped closer and squinted. The covers to every single one had been altered. Donkey ears and teeth were drawn on Alec's face in thick black marker. Like they'd done to people they thought were asses in high school.

She shuffled back a few steps, her mouth falling open. Ten covers stared back at her with Alec's donkey face.

Alec stepped into the gift shop and stood beside her, staring at the covers, too.

"Looks like you made someone angry." Valerie's voice wavered, unsure what the hell was happening.

"Yes," Alec said, "someone who means something to me." He touched her arm, forced her to turn to him. "Sometimes you need to be able to admit you're an ass."

"Wait, you did this?" Valerie's throat was thick.

"It's my apology if you'll accept it." His hands were open at his sides. "I was an ass. I'm sorry."

Their old joke had been turned around, flipped into something much larger. Something she never saw coming. Her heart seemed to pole-vault over her ribs. The sweet feeling of knowing everything had the possibility to be okay again lulled her like a bath. She let herself float there for a moment, until she remembered she didn't deserve to feel relief. Why was he the only one apologizing? She needed to apologize, too.

He pointed at the wilting flowers in her hand. "What are those?"

She'd forgotten she still had them. "I was going to *Pretty Woman* you," she explained. "Roses are hard to come by on short notice."

"You brought *me* flowers?" His mouth quirked up and displayed his dimple.

"What?" She stood up straighter. "You're the only one who's allowed to be sorry?"

"Typical Val." He stepped closer to her, his eyes not leaving hers. "Trying to steal the thunder of my apology."

"No, this is wow." She let herself fall back into the warm relief, and understand what his gesture really meant. He was willing to deface something he'd been so proud of, for the whole of their graduating class to see, for her. "It's just that I want to apologize, too. My pictures should be up there, also. Our fight this morning was as much my fault as it was yours."

"It was a little more your fault." He banged his hip against hers, the studs on his belt shiny in the overhead lights. "But I was willing to take one for the team."

"Careful," she chastised with a smile.

"I'm sure we could get some old yearbooks if you feel like you need to express yourself that way, but right now, if you're offering, 'I'm sorry' will do."

Laughter bubbled up at the same time tears did. "I'm sorry, I was an ass."

"You were," he said. "We both were." His arms circled her.

She nodded in agreement, allowing him to pull her in so his chin sat on her head.

"But just because we're both asses doesn't mean we can't be together, right?" he asked.

God, she hoped not. Valerie looked up at him. She needed to see him when that word came from his lips. "Say that again."

"Together," he repeated, and his brown eyes seemed as sure as his embrace.

"Just to clarify, you mean *together* together, like a couple?"

He laughed. "If you want me to be your boyfriend, if you are ready to say yes to being my girlfriend, then I'd be honored."

"Yes," she said, snuggling into him tighter.

"I want to be the man you count on," he whispered into the top of her head. "I always did, Valerie, I just didn't know it."

"How can this be so easy?" she gushed. She hadn't had to ask for it. He was offering it. Everything she'd wanted. He was willing to give it to her.

"I have a feeling it won't be," he said, "but I'm willing to deal with that, too, if you are."

She nodded against his chest and exhaled forcefully. Alec's arms were there to hold her up.

"I know I haven't always been the most forthcoming with

feelings and talking, but I'm going to give that a shot for you," he added.

"You're off to a pretty stupendous start."

He moved in, his lips aiming for a kiss that was bound to send them both spinning, but stopped and laid his cheek against hers. "Fuck, I want to kiss you right now, but I need to tell you I love you first. It's something I should have said a long time ago, something I never want to forget to tell you again."

"I love you," she said quickly. Saying it felt so natural. "And I should have told you a long time ago, too."

His mouth twisted. "You are seriously not making my sweeping you off your feet all that easy."

She cupped his chin. "Sorry, sweep away."

His eyes clung to hers. "I love you, Valerie."

She let the words hit her. He was saying them. Not singing them. Not whispering them. *Saying* them. Making sure she heard them. Making sure she knew. Speaking the unspoken that had been between them forever. He punctuated his words with a deep, blinding kiss.

She lost herself in his lips and tongue and promise until the other question from that morning smashed in her mind. She pulled back and swallowed. "What about London?" They'd said the unspoken, but London was still something they needed to discuss, *together, love* or not.

"We kept a long distance best friendship going for ten years, I think we can handle just one as a couple." He squeezed her tighter. "Don't you?"

She nodded, even as tears sprung anew. "I know it was stupid for me to say I wasn't going because of us. It's just that I am going to hate being away from you. Maybe you should come with me," she added, saying the words she'd come down here to say. She wanted Alec to know that she could ask him for forever, too. She could put herself out there, just like he had that day after graduation ten years ago.

"Yeah, I thought about that—maybe it's time for Chronic Disharmony to do a European tour."

There were no words to express her happiness at that statement, so she kissed him long and true, with lips and heart and breath she hoped would make up for years, for everything. She pulled back, a glance at his vandalized pictures bringing a fresh giggle. "What do we do now?"

The mischievous smile she loved graced his lips. "Cockfucius says…" He slipped his hand down and teased his finger at her waistband. "Go back upstairs and christen our fucking bed."

She laughed. "What about all the kisses we have to make up for?" They might be more than best friends now, but she would never stop giving him crap right back.

"We have forever for that now, Dirty Girl."

Forever, the word hit her just as his lips did. Sealing the promise of everything they could be, and everything they now were.

Epilogue

Alec headed backstage at the Royal Festival Hall in London. It was two months into Valerie's residency and he was just as excited to see her as he had been the first time he visited.

Backstage was bustling after the concert, held the same energy as backstage after one of his Chronic Disharmony shows. He and Valerie might have had different musical paths, different aspirations, but the buzz of putting on a good show was what they both chased.

They would always understand each other in that primal way.

He couldn't convince the guys to do a European tour, so he'd worked out being able to take his plane to visit Valerie once a month. It wasn't enough. It was never enough, but the way she looked like just-birthed sunlight was shooting from her skin when she took her final bow after a standing ovation, the way she seemed to float on that sunlight when she played her current solo, let him know her career was worth their separation.

Besides, it was only ten more months, 300 more days, 7305

more hours, 438,290 minutes, but who was counting?

He was. He thought back to the night at the reunion when he'd put her to sleep counting kisses. Even then, even after, during the days and nights they spent together before she left for London, he never felt like he had kissed her enough. Nothing came close to making up for ten years. To proving how many more years he longed to spend with her—how many more kisses he couldn't wait to count into her waiting lips.

He stood outside her closed dressing room door, ran his fingers over the petals of the white roses he'd purchased, and checked the front of his tux jacket for lint. He left his rock star clothes at home when he came to see Valerie at the symphony. He wanted to dress with the respect she deserved for playing at this level.

The last time he visited and waited outside her dressing room in a tux, with flowers in hand, he couldn't help equating it with picking her up for their prom. He was finally dressed as the man she'd always waited for. He was finally the man he'd always wanted to be.

He tucked the ring box deeper into his pocket and took a deep breath. This was the final piece. He was going to ask Valerie to marry him over breakfast in bed tomorrow with the smell of coffee in the air and nothing but their lives in front of them.

He would finally be her forever, and she would be his.

That wasn't his only surprise. The house he bought for his mother had sold and he was using the money to buy a vacation home for him and Valerie in Napa—their own little cottage where they could get away from the world.

Valerie was the only woman he needed to take care of now.

He knocked and entered Valerie's dressing room, the roses leading the way. She was sitting at her vanity, running a brush through her long brown hair. Upon seeing him in the reflection of the mirror, she ran to him, grabbed the roses, and hugged him tight. The feel of her, the way her curves fit his lines, the smell of her like a millions roses, the two of them lost and found in one embrace.

When he was with her, no matter where they were, he was home.

"You don't have to bring roses every time you come to see me." Her eyes shone. "You are enough."

He stole a glance at her dress—black, velvet, and off the shoulder. He knew she'd be wearing a bustier and black lace panties underneath. He couldn't wait to slide her stockings down, nuzzle and lick the creamy skin of her thighs.

He kissed her shoulder. "I'm never going to stop *Pretty Woman*-ing you. Besides, you're in the symphony. Roses are like ties." He smirked. "Required."

She tossed a smirk right back. "Red roses," she corrected.

"Damn, I always have to be a little off, don't I?"

"I wouldn't want you any other way." She kissed him long and hard—their lips singing a song, telling a story, living a life.

He still couldn't believe he'd denied himself this for ten years, her for ten years. His proposal would end that denial for good.

She pulled back and gazed at him. Her swollen mouth made his cock jerk to life. "And in that tuxedo you are perfection." She sighed.

"Wait until you see me out of it." He pressed a hand to her back and kissed her again, fast forwarding to when they would be in her tiny apartment by the River Thames. The lights of the city twinkling outside her window as his hands explored every bit of her, his lips tracing and trailing every curve and crevice. His cock had found a home, too. Just like he longed for Valerie, it longed for her. When he was with her, familiarity and surprise intermingled in a way that drove him wild. Made him crave what he knew and what he couldn't wait to find out.

"What are you thinking about?" she asked. Maybe she could read his mind, maybe she was also fast-forwarding.

"You." He tipped her chin up. "Making love to you, all night long." *Hearing the word "yes" from your lips tomorrow morning when I ask you the question that will end all the questions I've ever had.*

"All night long?" Her lips twitched. "That doesn't sound very ambitious. You're here for the whole weekend."

He laughed and kissed her again. His tongue wrapped around that familiar taste—peppermint and Valerie—sharpness and musky heat. She pressed her tits into his chest, and his lips skipped down to sample the sumptuous line of her cleavage.

Fuck, a weekend wasn't even long enough. He wanted to make love to her forever. If they could get away with fucking every minute for the rest of their lives, he'd be up for it—spending eternity in bed with his Valerie, his Dirty Girl, his everything.

He supposed his proposal was the first step. But was it perfect, yet? He loved her apartment, but a replay of the weekend they fell in love would be even better.

He shifted his lips to her ear. "I have an idea," he said, the heat of it exciting him even further, "how about we get a hotel this weekend?"

"Are you sick of my apartment already?"

"I was thinking we should try to christen every rented bed in London that we can while you're living here."

Her body shuddered in a laugh. "We have a lot of work ahead of us. Do you know how many hotels are in London?"

His eyes roved over her lips, those swollen flute-player lips. "That's a challenge I'm willing to undertake."

"I think you're going to have to come and visit more than

once a month."

"Don't tempt me."

She ran a finger along the collar of his shirt. "That, along with loving you, is my only job."

Alec had never thought he deserved that kind of attention, that kind of love, but now he didn't question it because it was fully reciprocated—a mirror of feeling, of love, of lust. Everything he gave her, she reflected back.

She rushed her hand down and cupped his cock. "We better check in soon, or the ice and vending area here doesn't stand a chance."

He stiffened even more under her touch. "Dirty Girl, when I'm with you, nowhere stands a chance."

She grabbed her things and they headed through the backstage corridors and out into the London night. They had a whole weekend ahead of them, a whole world ahead of them—Al and Val.

They were inseparable besties and now insatiable lovers. As people had said back in high school, one was never without the other.

He palmed the ring he'd gotten for her and knew that would always be true.

About the Author

Candy Sloane is a pseudonym for a Young Adult & New Adult author who needed to write some naughty books her mother couldn't read. She lives in Portland, OR and loves Lifetime movies.

Also by Candy Sloane

THE REALITY O

If you love sexy romance, one-click these steamy Brazen releases…

FALLING FOR HIS BEST FRIEND
an *Out of Uniform* novella by Katee Robert

Staring down a surgery that'll change her life, Avery Yeung's running out of time to get knocked up. And the only guy within donating distance? Her overprotective—and irritatingly hot—best friend. While daddyhood is pretty much the last thing he wants, Drew Flannery won't let Avery shop for a "popsicle pop." Between the bed, the kitchen counter, and against his squad car, Avery and Drew are having the hottest sex *ever*. And they can't get enough of it—or each other. Or notice that they've crossed the one line that could ruin their friendship forever…

EMERGENCY ENGAGEMENT
a *Love Emergency* novel by Samanthe Beck

Savannah Smith expected a marriage proposal—just not from the super-hot next-door neighbor who she just knocked out with a paint can. But when their families catches them in a compromising position, everyone assumes he's "The One" Savannah's been talking about. Beau Montgomery can't bring himself to ruin his mother's "Christmas miracle," but after the crushing losses in his past, he won't risk putting himself out there again. A fake engagement for the holidays is the perfect plan. If, of course, they don't fall in love first…

TIE ME DOWN TIGHT
a *Breaking the Rules* novella by Cathryn Fox

The last thing Hollywood heavyweight Dylan Brooks wants is to dress up like a cowboy and attend a party for some chick he doesn't know. But when the sweet girl with the angelic face looks at him like she wants to eat him alive, he pulls out his lasso and ties her down tight. Dylan asks for one week of fun, and Angie Stanton can't resist. But she won't fall again for an actor, no matter how tempting he might be. And she's not the only one with trust issues…

ONE NIGHT OF SCANDAL
an *After Hours* novel by Elle Kennedy

Newly single teacher Darcy Grant is tired of walking the straight and narrow path. She's on the hunt for passion, and there's no denying ex-fighter Reed Miller is just the man to give it to her. There's only one problem—Reed is her ex's best friend. Now it's just a matter of setting a few ground rules…and hoping her rule-breaking, sweet-talking bad boy agrees to follow them. But if she lets Reed into her bed, does she stand a chance of keeping him out of her heart?

CPSIA information can be obtained
at www.ICGtesting.com
Printed in the USA
BVHW032126020420
576763BV00001B/17